VALERIE

In the long run

Published by
Llyfrau Cambria Books, Wales, United Kingdom.
Cambria Books is a division of
Cambria Publishing.
Discover our other books at: www.cambriabooks.co.uk

For my husband, Chris Norris

Chapter 1

The eruption of the ten girls into the Lounge, teetering in their high-heeled shoes, was like a flock of exotic birds landing. Couples who were eating their meals paused, forks half way to their mouths, and muttered asides to each other. The rather military looking gentleman smoking a cigar at the end of the bar straightened his jacket with a firm tug, so that the brass buttons twitched. The middle-aged woman, who was all decked out in a red dress with green polka dots and sitting on a bar stool next to him, drew herself up and looked down her nose at them over the rim of her gin and tonic.

'What shall we have to drink? Do you think they have wine?'

'Ooh, I hope so. Let's have a couple of bottles.'

'Or three, or four.'

'I'd prefer a lager and lime.'

'My sash is falling off. Look, yours is too. It's from where we were squashed up in the minibus. You can't read what it says if it's all crushed up.'

They all smoothed out their pink sashes until the words 'Nicola's Hen Party' became clear.

'Ladies, what's your pleasure? Drinks-wise, that is.'

The barman was slim, dapper and sure of himself. He straightened his tie and placed his hands on the bar, sweeping his eyes over them, lingering here and there where a glitzy dress clung.

'Cheeky! We'll start with a bottle of your house white wine, two lager and limes and two gin and tonics.'

'Where's the lovely bride?' This was said over his shoulder as he deftly twisted the corkscrew into the first bottle. 'Ah, there she is.' Nicola was standing at the back of the group, a white shoulder length veil and a plastic tiara askew on her head. 'What a crime for us lads, you

1

being out of circulation.'

Nicola tittered behind her hand, a flush coming into her plump cheeks. She pulled a pack of cigarettes out of her bag.

One of the girls looked round at the half a dozen meals that were being eaten. 'The food looks good. We could eat here before we go into town. Nicola, it's your night, what do you think?'

Nicola shrugged. 'I don't mind. You're organising it all, Lou.'

Louise didn't answer straightaway because she was busy sorting out the money for the drinks from a bulging purse that she was carrying. Five-pound notes unfurled as she delved into it.

Sounds of Bohemian Rhapsody drifted in from the juke-box in the bar.

'Oh I love this record! Is it still number 1 this week? Shouldn't we head straight for the clubs and start dancing?' This was said by a willowy blonde while she gyrated to the music, arms above her head. The middle-aged woman on the bar stool shook her head and made a remark to her gentleman companion.

Louise shook her head decisively. 'No, this one needs some food inside her first.' She jerked her head at Nicola, who was struggling to light her cigarette. 'Can we have some menus, please?'

The barman handed them a pile of well-thumbed sheets with 'Home cooking at its best' written across the top. 'I think the kitchen was just closing but the guvnor might make an exception for you lovely ladies'.

The guvnor, who was slightly tubby and shirtsleeved, did indeed make an exception for them. He stood at the girls' table, genial and smiling, pen in hand ready to write their order on his notepad while they wondered how to choose between scampi and chips, a nice juicy steak, sausage and mash or a few other pub favourites.

He carried their order off with him and handed it to a short-haired, slim young woman wearing an apron with a tea towel tucked into the belt. She was standing at the bar with her hands on her hips. Out the corner of her eye (because most of her attention was on Nicola, who was looking distinctly wobbly on her chair) Louise caught the pantomime that was going on. The short-haired woman frowned at the order and shook her head, pointing at the clock. The landlord jerked his head back over his shoulder to their table and tried to get the woman to take the piece of paper.

Oh no, thought Louise. What shall I do now? She sighed. There's a lot of responsibility comes with this matron of honour business, she thought. She was just about to go and plead with them when the woman snatched the order and strode off. Louise hoped it was to the kitchen.

The food, when it came, was good. The chips were nice and crispy and Lou's steak was done exactly as she had ordered. When she paid the bill out of the big purse of money containing all the girls' contributions she passed onto the landlord how much they'd enjoyed the meal. Then she thanked him for keeping the kitchen open and asked him if he would he pass their thanks on to the cook? He beamed, and said he hoped that they would enjoy the rest of their evening and that they would come again. She wondered briefly if he actually would tell the aproned woman, who was now nowhere to be seen. She didn't dwell on it though, because now there was the challenge of getting Nicola out to the minibus.

In the car-park, while Louise was holding Nicola's hair back for her to throw up behind the minibus, she looked up at the pub sign. *The Spinning Coins*. Yes, I may well come here again, she thought.

*

The January morning was struggling. Daylight appeared reluctantly and the sky remained obstinately grey. The light was yellow in the tiny kitchenette as Kitty plugged the kettle in and spooned Nescafé into her cup. She pushed open the casement window to sample the air, and it rushed in to greet her, bracing and fresh. But not too cold, she thought, pulling it shut. I won't need a fleece layer under my jacket.

She had already taken a cup of tea and the *Daily Mirror* in to Rob, who had been lying on his back as usual, snoring gently. He had grunted his thanks as she put the cup down on the bedside table, and she picked up his shirt, boxer shorts and socks from last night and dropped them in the laundry basket. Sometimes it was easier just to do it.

She continued her morning routine by going back to the kitchen and putting two Weetabix and sugar in a bowl and topping it off with milk. She had heard, with her ear well attuned to the normal morning sounds, that Danny was out of the bathroom and – hopefully – getting himself dressed. If that process took too long she would go and divert him from reading his comics or playing with his toys to the less interesting task of getting his clothes on. Today, however, he appeared promptly.

'You're going to play with Luke today, aren't you?' she asked as she pulled his sweater down tidily.

He nodded abstractedly, wriggled away from her ministrations and sat down to crush his Weetabix down into the milk with his spoon. He was humming away to himself. Kitty looked at her son, absorbed as he was in his own little world. She had the urge to hug him and smother him with kisses. While he would tolerate it, she knew it wouldn't be welcome so she contented herself by just looking at him, soaking up every fold and curve of him.

'Is Dad awake?'

'I took him his cup of tea and the paper, but he might have dozed off again.'

'Can I take my breakfast and have it with Granny then, downstairs?'

'She might not be there this morning. She's probably still in her cottage.'

'But I just heard her. I heard her talking.'

'Did you indeed?' Kitty knew what that meant.

Danny glanced at his mother's face. 'I won't annoy her. Honestly.'

Kitty swept up some stray crumbs from the worktop, where Rob had made a late night sandwich before coming to bed. 'She never is annoyed with you. Alright, go on then. I'll come too.'

Kitty left Danny to carry the bowl of cereal down the stairs himself, because he wanted to be a big boy, with a warning not to spill it. She herself went into the Bar. It was a smallish room at the back of the pub, with the walls painted the unimaginative cream that the brewery deemed appropriate. Kitty had hung pictures of country scenes to brighten it up, and she thought it worked well enough. There were a dozen or so tables, some the small round ones, seating three customers or four if they were good enough friends to squash up. The other tables were square wooden affairs designed for bigger parties and for meals, although it was mostly in the Lounge for food. Even though the chairs and stools (stools took up less space) were upended on the tables and the floor still glistening wet from recent mopping, the smell of stale beer from last night, and thirty years of last nights, still clung. She threw a couple of windows open and went into the Lounge. Here the intention was to convey smartness and comfort, which it achieved to a fairly good standard with a plush but serviceable carpet and upholstered seating. A good deal of well-polished brass completed the effect. A lavishly decorated Christmas tree, with a puddle of green needles beneath it, occupied a corner by the fireplace, and in the fireplace and hearth there was still ash from last night's fire. A vacuum cleaner stood alone in the middle of the room like an exhibit in a museum.

Hands on hips, Kitty surveyed the scene. The room had been vacuumed, after a fashion, to half way across, like a tide mark on a beach. In the other half the detritus of a busy evening still littered the carpet – the odd cigarette butt, crumbs, dirt brought in on shoes, dropped food, crumpled napkins. She went down on her hands and knees at the fireplace, took the poker from the brass companion set on the hearth and vigorously riddled the ashes through the grate. Then she took up the little brush and cleaned off the hearth, marvelling that it was really so difficult to grasp that it was best to do this dusty task before vacuum cleaning.

She hadn't heard anyone come in until there was a voice behind her. 'Oh, it's you. I thought it would be Rob.'

Still on her knees and brush in hand, Kitty said 'Good morning to you too, Doris. I don't suppose you'd know where Maisie is? The vacuum cleaner looks rather abandoned.' She didn't try too hard to keep the sarcasm out of her voice.

Doris drew her cardigan around her and looked Kitty in the eye. 'You know we like a bit of a morning chat now and again.'

'Would that be with a bit of tea and toast and a half hour break for Maisie?'

Doris opened her mouth to reply just as Danny came in, carefully balancing his bowl of Weetabix and milk, his face puckered with concentration.

'Well, if it isn't my little lamb,' said Doris, in the cooing voice she

5

kept specially for Danny. 'Here, let Granny carry that for you. In fact, why don't you let me make you a nice dish of porridge instead. Much better of a winter morning'

'I'll take it,' said Kitty, jumping up and practically snatching the dish from Danny's hands. 'And he asked for Weetabix.' She whisked it into the kitchen where Maisie was sitting at the small table in the corner, a piece of toast half way to her mouth. She dropped it back onto her plate and shifted on her stool. Toast crumbs decorated the front of her overall. She nodded rather than spoke her good morning.

'Sit you down here,' said Doris to Danny, pulling a stool out while she plonked her own bulk down on a stool next to him. 'More tea, Maisie?' She picked up the fat black tea pot that stood on the table.

Kitty turned and went back to the Lounge before she could hear any more. She turned her attention to the Christmas tree, where it stood patiently in the corner. Other Christmas decorations - lanterns, baubles, streamers – dangled limply from the ceiling.

'I thought you'd all left me on my own up there,' said Rob from behind her. He was in a tee-shirt, despite the January morning. He never seemed to feel the cold. It's due to the layer the fat on him, thought Kitty. It runs in the family. Rob swigged from the mug of tea he was carrying and came over to put his arm round Kitty and give her a kiss, his dark stubble rasping her cheek. 'Alright, love? What are you staring at?' he followed her gaze. 'Have we got a mouse in the Christmas tree or something?'

'They're at it again,' hissed Kitty in a whisper. 'Maisie and your mother. We don't pay Maisie to drink tea and eat toast when the cleaning's only half done.'

Rob dropped his arm from her and sat down on one of the upholstered bench seats that ran around the edge of the room. He picked up a beer mat and twirled it between his fingers. 'Oh, Maisie always gets it all done. I don't see that a cup of tea hurts.'

'I've got no problem with that, but not before the cleaning's finished. She only does half a job as it is.' When Rob didn't reply – it wasn't the first time they'd had this discussion – Kitty added, 'And these Christmas decorations. They can come down today. Look, the tree's past its best and decorations always look pathetic once you're into

6

January.' She looked pointedly at Rob's cup. 'If everyone's got time to sit around drinking tea then they have time to do this.' She nodded at the kitchen. 'I'll go and tell the two witches out there'.

Kitty marched in and announced the plan. Doris sucked her teeth and shook her head gravely. 'Oh no, you can't do that. The decorations have to stay up until Twelfth Night else it's bad luck. It's only Friday today and Twelfth Night's, what, Monday? Is that right, Mais?'

'Er, I'm not sure,' said Maisie, blinking rapidly behind her glasses.

'Daddy!' said Danny suddenly. He leapt up from the table and threw himself at Rob, who was hovering gingerly in the kitchen doorway.

'Hello mate!' Rob scooped him up, part hug, part wrestle, while Danny whooped in delight. Rob groaned and held his back theatrically as he put him down. 'You're getting too big for me to throw you around now, boy.'

'You are a big lad and all,' said Maisie from her corner. 'Let's see, how old are you now?'

'Eight,' said Danny still holding onto his dad and looking up at him adoringly.

Kitty picked up a fresh dishcloth and wiped the new stainless steel kitchen worktops, even though they had been cleaned last night. She knew that for sure because she'd done it herself.

'We were just talking about taking the Christmas decorations down today rather than waiting for Twelfth Night on Monday,' she said to Rob as she wiped. 'Everyone's sick of Christmas decorations now and the pub will look fresher without them. And,' she pointed at him for emphasis, 'there's more time today. Saturday and Sunday morning, I'll be working in the kitchen and Monday Danny's back in school.'

Doris sniffed. 'Well, back in our day we always left the decorations up until Twelfth Night, no matter what. It's traditional and the customers expected it. But of course you can do what you like.'

Rob looked cautiously between his mother and his wife, the agony of his dilemma written all over his face.

'Well,' he said, attempting a weak smile, 'We probably shouldn't break with tradition. And there'll be plenty of time after Danny's gone to school on Monday, Kitkat.' The look he gave her was a mixture of apology and appeal.

Danny had picked up his Nintendo Game Boy, his favourite Christmas present, and his thumbs were flying over the controls. Without lifting his eyes from the screen he said, 'I like the Christmas tree. I wish it could stay there forever.'

Abruptly Kitty turned her back on them all and went to stand by the kitchen window. Outside the road was gleaming and shiny from the light overnight rain. Outside the clouds were starting to lift as if the sky drew breath. Outside the wet road curved around the corner and disappeared tantalisingly out of sight. Suddenly, she couldn't wait another second.

*

Kitty had been running grimly for a couple of hundred yards or so before she remembered that she hadn't done her customary stretching. She stopped and pushed with her hands against the side wall of the tiny village Post Office while she pushed her calf muscles back, one leg at a time, and felt the lengthening down the whole back of her leg. The she stood on one leg, stork-like, pressed her foot into her buttock and eased out her thigh muscles, three times for each leg. Finally, she finished off the short routine with a few squats. The familiar movements served to calm her and she set off again at a more reasonable pace, winding through the village, passing *Clarke's Family Butchers* with its swinging sign on her right and the small baker's plus a hairdresser's on her left. Finally, their rival pub, *The Bear*, marked the end of the main street before the last straggle of buildings petered out. The church and primary school were off down a lane to the left. It wasn't the prettiest village you could imagine, no village green or duck pond or anything, but the bus service wasn't bad and it was home.

A car going past beeped its horn at her and she automatically smiled and waved back. From the quick glimpse that she got she vaguely recognised one of the lads who frequented the bar several nights a week. She could never get their names off pat. But just remember, they are our bread and butter, Rob would say.

Just outside of the village she veered off to the right, down a track alongside a field where sleepy sheep chewed grass indifferently. The rutted track had many puddles, and she splashed through them doggedly, almost relishing the cold muddy water splashing over her

8

Lycra leggings. Just once, she thought, couldn't he take my side just once? Another voice in her head said, she knows she can wind you up. You know it too. So don't let her. Her feet rhythmically drummed the earth, her pace automatic and familiar, while her mind replayed the morning scene and she rewrote the script with several different scenarios, mostly involving a good stand-up row with her mother-in-law.

She took an offshoot track through the trees to the right, which you could easily overlook if you didn't know all these paths like the back of your hand, as Kitty did. She knew all the distances too: another three miles back to *The Spinning Coins* by this route, making a four mile run altogether. And now for the hill climb. A steep ascent up the side of the ridge, coming at just the right time in the run, after she was nicely warmed up. She felt her heartbeat and breathing respond to the increased physical challenge as she pumped her arms and lowered her head like a stubborn bull. Dig in, was her mantra, dig in. The repetition of the words filled her mind, blocking out everything else. She pushed even harder than usual today and she was gasping and sweating by the time she reached the top. This was always the sublime moment, this moment when she burst out from the trees onto the summit, the ridge conquered. Her Rocky moment. It was the only time she voluntarily stopped on a run, here, right here, where the land below surrendered itself to her, and the river cut a silver trail in the valley. It was a mere minute or so that she allowed herself, but it was enough. She was lightheaded after the punishing climb, and with the lens of her being open to allow the co-mingling of the machine that was her body with the natural world around her. Thoughts and words were not enough, and she didn't seek them.

Today a movement on a nearby post caught her eye and a cheeky robin was watching her with alert, knowing eyes. Kitty couldn't help smiling. How could you not? She allowed herself to appreciate the pulsation of vigour through her body in this special place, today complete with robin, for another few seconds. Then her thoughts, along with her feet, started to return homeward. She's going to get her way, she thought, those bloody decorations will stay up until Monday. But I don't suppose it really matters. And Rob's always been under his mother's thumb so nothing was going to be different this morning. I shouldn't have stormed out like that. I'll say sorry to Rob. Yes, that's what I'll do. But I'm not saying sorry to *her*.

She had turned back onto the main road now and she could see the pub, the sign with the five gold coins swaying slightly on its hinges. Her mind turned to the cooking she needed to do this morning. A batch of individual fish pies and lasagnes to put in the freezer.

But where was the letter? Surely it should be here by now.

*

You needed a pullover under your jacket on the first day back at the office after the Christmas holidays, because the heating had been off for all those days. Malcolm knew this only too well and he hunted through the drawer of ironed and folded woollies to find the thickest one that he could. No tie today though. He'd save that for when the university got back into full swing. This would be when the undergraduates came back, but this wasn't until next week. Thank goodness.

He heard the sound of the bathroom door closing and Celia's tread on the stairs. He lingered in the bedroom, checking his briefcase, glancing briefly at the book on the bedside table that he had been reading last night, pulling back the curtains and glancing out into the sedate cul-de-sac. Various familiar kitchen noises drifted up to him; the laying of plates and knives on the table, the kettle boiling, the fridge door closing. When he heard the toast pop up in the toaster he picked up his belongings and went downstairs.

Celia's back was to him as he entered the kitchen. She put the toast into a rack and joined him where he was sat at the table.

'I'll put the radio on, shall I?'

Celia nodded. She was engrossed in pouring coffee from the cafetiere into two mugs. She was wearing a pink quilted dressing gown and her face, bare of makeup as it was, looked pale and closed in the harsh glare of the kitchen light.

'Did you manage to sleep, darling? I heard you get up several times.'

Her eyes flickered up briefly from where she was spreading butter on toast. 'I came downstairs to read for a while.' Then she added, after a pause, 'And you?'

'I had a bit of trouble getting off. A lot of things kept running through my head, especially with going back to work this morning.'

The interview that was being broadcast on Radio 4's Today programme hung in the room. Malcolm tried to concentrate on it but the words slid past his brain.

'Well,' he said after he had finished his toast and drained his coffee. 'I'd better get going.' He got his overcoat from the hallstand and came back to say goodbye. 'I won't be very late tonight. Around six, I should think.'

He felt himself being scrutinised. 'Aren't you going to take your new scarf?'

He tutted. 'Ah, of course. How could I have forgotten my new Christmas present?' He ran nimbly upstairs and, after a few moments of searching, reappeared with a red scarf round his neck.

'I'll see you later,' he said, at the threshold of the kitchen. 'I hope you have a good day.' For a moment he thought she was going to get up to see him off, but when she didn't, he went to her and bent down to kiss her cheek. The tendrils of her fair hair tickled his face.

As he closed the door of his BMW he selected Radio 4, but then changed his mind and tuned to Radio 3. A piece by Herbert Howells was being played. Malcolm recalled that he had written the piece after his young son died. He turned the volume up until it filled the car and reverberated in his skull.

*

Celia took the plates, mugs and cutlery and loaded them into the dishwasher. Then she went back upstairs and had a long hot shower. Afterwards she rubbed Crabtree and Evelyn lavender body lotion into her water-softened limbs. She slipped back into her dressing gown while the lotion soaked in, then made the bed and selected a turtle necked cashmere sweater and soft woollen trousers, both size 16 from Marks and Spencer. She fastened on her gold wristwatch and pearl earrings. When she went back downstairs she turned the radio off and made herself a second cup of coffee – instant this time. She sat again at the kitchen table to drink it. Her eyes moved to the clock, its heavy tick audible in the quiet kitchen. It was half-past nine.

Chapter 2

Today Kitty took a different route, more suited to doing a longer run. She cut down the narrow footpath along the side of the pub car-park which then took her across the field beyond. The night had left the grass with a delicate sugar coating of frost which crunched pleasingly under her feet. The winter morning sun sent her shadow, as long as a giant, sprawling across the land in front of her. She waved her arms up and down, and smiled as she saw the shadow jerk, puppet-like, in response. Birds were singing and the church bell had started tolling to welcome in the Sunday worshippers. It was, quite simply, a splendid winter morning.

Now, which route should she take? I could do thirteen miles, she thought. No, be sensible, came the countering thought. You haven't run thirteen miles since that half marathon in the autumn. Better to start with twelve today, and then gradually increase the mileage week by week. I must work out a schedule. How many weeks have I got? Let's see, it's January the fifth today...

But counting the weeks without a calendar in front of her was hard, and her thoughts instead went back to Friday morning, to when she had got back to the pub after her run, resigned to Doris having her way and the Christmas decorations staying up, resigned to a morning cooking in the kitchen, resigned, almost, to the routine of life as a pub landlord's wife. She had panted up the stairs to their flat above the pub, peeling off her jacket as she went, and there was Rob, standing on the landing with a tentative smile on his face and one hand behind his back.

'It's come', he said, and produced the letter from behind his back with a flourish. 'This is it, isn't it? From London. It got delivered to the cottage by mistake yesterday, and Ma's just brought it round.'

Kitty took it and gazed at her name on the envelope. Yes, this was it. She was going to know at last. Her fingers were sweaty and cumbersome, and the thumping of her heart wasn't only the aftermath of running. 'You do it.' She passed it back to Rob.

He tore open the envelope without hesitation. She watched his eyes following the words on the page. He blinked. 'Well, I think it means...'

She snatched the letter from him. And there it was, in black and white. She took a deep breath. 'I've got in. I've actually got in! I'm going to run the London Marathon on 12 April.'

*

Kitty smiled as she climbed over a stile and entered the wood, remembering the pandemonium that had broken out after she had made her announcement. Rob had whooped and hugged her, and they did a crazy dance together across the kitchen. Danny had actually put down his Gameboy and come in to see what all the noise was about.

'A marathon,' he had said, his eyes round with wonder. 'Is that a very long way?'

'Oh yes,' said Kitty, ruffling his hair. 'It's more than twenty-six miles. Like from here to where we go to the cinema.'

'Wow,' said Danny. 'Can you really run all that way?'

'Well, I hope so...' She paused. Twenty-six miles. Twenty-six point two, to be exact. That would take at least three-quarters of an hour in the car. She turned to Rob. 'Oh my God, Rob, that's twice as far as I've ever run so far. What if I can't do it?'

He kissed her on the cheek. 'Of course you can do it. Look how fit you are.' He ran his hands over her back and bottom. 'And not an ounce of fat anywhere. Unlike me.'

She kissed him back warmly on the mouth. To be fair, he was supportive of her running, and boasted about her whenever he had the chance. And she didn't mind that he was slightly overweight; he was lovely to cuddle up to.

'Yuk,' said Danny in response to their kissing and took himself back to his bedroom, closing the door.

Rob ran his hands over Kitty's hips. 'Didn't you say Danny's going to Tina's to play with Luke this afternoon? How about a little siesta when we close up after lunch?'

Kitty put her arms round his neck, the letter still clutched in her hand. 'Alright, then. And I won't be all sweaty then like I am now.'

Rob burrowed his hand up inside her top. 'Sweaty or not, I don't care either way.'

Kitty closed her eyes. He might be under his mother's thumb sometimes, but not all the time.

*

After about half a mile of crossing the field, over a stile and into woodland, she came to a car-park. At least, it was a clearing in the woods for about a dozen cars, with a rubbish bin, a rusting bench and a notice reminding you to lock your car. It was a favourite spot for dog walkers and she always had to be careful where she put her feet. You learned by experience that dogs had to relieve themselves as soon as they bounded out of the car, and that their owners often didn't notice. Or pretended not to.

There were two cars in the car-park this morning. One was a battered old estate that she saw regularly, sometimes just when it was decanting three big dogs, deliriously excited at the prospect of freedom. The other one caught her eye because it seemed out of place in the woods. It was a four-door large saloon car, cream and sumptuous. Although Kitty's knowledge of cars was minimal, she recognised this as stylish. A million miles away from their serviceable but old Ford Escort, which was regularly laden with goods from the Cash & Carry.

A man had his back to her, locking the door of the cream car. He was wearing Lycra leggings, trainers and a light jacket, and was jogging gently on the spot. Although she liked to run solo – it gave her precious alone time, time away from the busy pub routine – she always felt a welcome camaraderie when she saw a fellow runner. When he turned round she was surprised to see he was wearing a red woolly scarf around his neck. Surely he'd get too hot with that? Don't stare, she thought. She dropped her eyes and said a quick hello as she passed.

'Excuse me.' She turned round. 'I, um, I wonder if you can help me,' he said. 'Do you know these woods around here?' He nodded at the surroundings.

'Yes, very well.' She had uncapped her water bottle and taken a swig. She noticed he carried a water bottle too which he was fingering. 'Where do you want to get to?'

He laughed nervously. 'Well, I don't know, really. I think you can get down to the canal from here?'

She nodded. 'You can indeed. It's about a mile from here. The towpath is great for running, and not usually too muddy underfoot.' She indicated the track up ahead. 'That will take you right to it, and those other two paths over there go to the canal too but they're longer.' She closed her water bottle, aware that the timer that she had set on her watch when she left the pub was ticking. 'Have a good run,' she said. He thanked her, and she nodded a goodbye and set off again.

After a few minutes she looked back over her shoulder, but the man with the red scarf was nowhere to be seen.

*

Rob gave a quick look down at his shirt front as he headed from the flat downstairs to the pub. Kitty was always telling him off for dropping food down his front and not noticing. But he could look and still not see what her sharp eyes would pick out, so he didn't bother to look too closely. He was pleasantly surprised to hear a cheerful hubbub from downstairs. As always, except for the one night a week he had off, Sam had opened up the pub for him at six o'clock prompt while Rob enjoyed a family tea upstairs with Kitty and Danny. The deal was that Sam looked after the Lounge and Bar on his own until Rob came down at about seven, but Sam would buzz on the intercom from behind the bar into the flat if it got busy before that.

Rob breezed into the Bar to find that the regular group of lads, six of them tonight, were playing a game of darts accompanied by much catcalling and cheering. Rob joined the group for a few minutes, chatting amiably while noticing with satisfaction that they all had fresh pints which didn't appear to be their first. The bills had to be paid and they always had the choice to go to *The Bear* down the road or, God forbid, go straight home to their wives after work. He also called a cheery 'alright, boys?' to three elderly men in the corner, more regulars, who sat in their overcoats in a fug of cigarette smoke, eking out their ale or their Guinness and not talking much.

Next Rob went behind the bar and into the Lounge side where Sam was efficiently pulling a pint of dark to go with the half of lager that already stood on the counter. 'Evening, guv,' he said. 'Alright?' Rob returned the greeting and cast his eye round his domain on the Lounge side. The middle aged half-of-lager-and-pint-of-dark couple were already perusing the menu. Another couple were sat at a table similarly making their meal choices, with two large glasses of wine on their table. And of course the Major stood at the end of the bar, a regular feature, his brass buttons gleaming and cravat neatly knotted. He would probably have his regular pint of bitter followed by two single-malt whiskey chasers. Or maybe three.

A good start for midweek, noted Rob. But then, you never could tell. Sometimes it could start off like this then by nine o'clock it was dead. Or, sometimes nothing until half past nine then suddenly, out of nowhere, in they all troop. He recalled the night recently when that hen party had come, all wanting meals. Still, they had spent a lot on food and drink even though he'd had to take a bucket of water out to wash away the sick in the car-park next morning. No, you never could tell.

What's more, he'd heard rumours about Sam and one of those hen party girls. A quickie in the ladies' toilets, by all accounts. He watched now as two young women came in and Sam came up to serve them, all swagger and smarm. It seemed like he just couldn't help himself. But Rob couldn't grumble about him as a barman. He worked at least forty hours a week, was always amiable and didn't short-change the customers. Rob knew he was lucky to have him.

Sam rang the bell on the bar, so that it sounded down the passage into the kitchen. Kitty appeared promptly, wiping her hand on her apron as she came up behind the bar.

Sam was busy scribbling on his pad. 'We've got two faggots and peas here, and another order for one hotpot and one beef curry. A small portion of chips instead of rice, though, and not too spicy with the curry.'

Kitty grunted. 'It'll come how a made it. I can't take the curry powder out now. If they want to be fussy they should stay at home.' She glanced sideways at Rob but he hadn't heard her.

Sam held up his hands. 'Don't blame me.' Kitty grabbed the orders. 'Just see if you could push the fish pie, would you Sam? There's just two portions left, it won't keep 'til tomorrow and there's no room in the freezer.'

16

'Phew,' said Sam to Rob when Kitty had flounced off to the kitchen. 'Wrong time of the month?'

'Oh, Kit's alright,' said Rob over his shoulder as he ran a cloth over the counter. 'Maybe there's been a bit of hassle upstairs.' He knew that Doris had popped in to say goodnight to Danny a few minutes before Kitty had come down to open the kitchen, and at those times he tended to find that he needed to come down to the pub to see that everything was going OK.

'Oh,' said Sam. 'Only Tess can turn into a right miserable cow when it's her time of the month.'

Rob eyed him. 'Well, Tess has a lot to put up with from you sometimes.'

Sam grinned. 'She knows which side her bread's buttered. And she knows it's her I love.' Rob shook his head. Water off a duck's back.

The Major was clearing his throat loudly. 'Another beer, my good sir?' said Rob, 'Or is it straight to the hard stuff?'

'Enough beer for one evening, I think. I'll have a double Glenfiddich, please. And one for yourself.'

'Very kind of you,' said Rob, measuring out the double and running a small jug of water to go on the side, just like the Major liked it. 'I'll take for a half.'

The Major placed the tumbler of whiskey exactly central on his beer mat and lined the jug up beside it. 'Is the Memsahib going to put in an appearance this evening?' he said, straightening his cravat.

'Couldn't tell you,' said Rob. 'Oh, wait a minute, she was upstairs with the boy just now, and she was quite dolled up, so I expect she will be.'

'Ah, jolly good,' beamed the Major, rubbing his hands.

'And speak of the devil,' Rob nodded his head towards the door.

Doris made her entrance. She must have had her hair done that day because it stood round her head like a silvery grey turban, and she was bejewelled wherever possible – ears, throat, wrists, fingers. The Major got off his bar stool and stood ramrod straight. 'Good evening, Doris,' he said. 'May I say that you are looking the picture of elegance tonight.'

Doris inclined her head and thanked him. He indicated with a flourish the bar stool next to his for her to join him and held her lightly under the elbow while she climbed on.

Rob watched this performance with approval. It was only right and decent that people looked smart in the Lounge, and Ma added a bit of class. She always had. 'Usual, Ma?' he said.

'Yes, please.' She cast her eye all around and Rob's eye followed hers, a quick trawl for empty glasses and abandoned ash trays that she might comment on. But tonight all she said was that it was nice and busy, before she turned to address some remark to the Major.

Rob poured her gin and tonic, which the Major paid for, and left them to their conversation. Yes, she was always well turned out, his Ma. A brief memory flashed through his mind of him as a boy, sitting on her bed in his pyjamas while she got ready for an evening behind the bar. On would go the rings, the lipstick, the perfume. Then before she went downstairs she would tell him to go to his own bed, where she would kiss him goodnight and tell him he could have the light on for half an hour, then he was to go to sleep like a good boy. Then she clicked down the stairs on her high heels and joined his Dad behind the bar. No meals, of course, in those days. Just crisps, peanuts and the jar of smoothly white pickled eggs that used to stand on the bar, and that fascinated him. Sometimes he would creep out of bed and listen at the top of the stairs to the loud voices and laughter wending up from the pub. Often he could pick out his father's voice and guffawing laugh. He could hear it now, as if it were yesterday.

*

Kitty noticed the car again when she ran through the car-park the following Sunday, but the owner with the red scarf was nowhere to be seen. She reflected briefly that presumably he must have been satisfied with his run if he had come back again. Then her mind shifted to other things. She wondered if she had prepared enough veg for the Sunday lunches before she set off. Anyway, Ivy was going to be coming in soon to finish off by doing the potatoes, as she did every Sunday. Kitty couldn't help fretting when she wasn't in charge in the kitchen, even though she knew that Ivy was perfectly capable. But would Ivy get the roast potatoes and Yorkshires nice and crisp? Would she make the gravy not too thick but not too thin either? She would have preferred to be doing the cooking herself as she did four lunchtimes and five evenings a week, but Rob said that on a Sunday lunchtime the wife of the landlord's place was beside him behind the bar, like in his Mum and Dad's day. So that's what she did.

Fourteen miles today; the weekly long run and the cornerstone of any marathon training. She allowed her body to settle in and enjoy the couple of hours ahead. After all, this was only a mile more than she had run in last year's half marathon. She pondered that as the weekly long run became longer and longer, she would have less time to get back, eat a second breakfast, shower and change before the pub opened at midday. The longest runs, the twenty milers, would take her, what, an hour longer than this fourteen mile one? She frowned, trying to work out the timings in her head. Well, I'll just have to make an earlier start, she concluded. I'll manage it somehow.

As she turned a corner in the woods to take one of the paths down to the canal she saw a man running some twenty yards in front of her. He was quite lanky, with greying hair. She wondered if he was the cream-car-red-scarf man, but there was no sign of the red scarf today and she hadn't really noticed the previous week what his hair was like, although she had had the impression that he wasn't young. The gap between them remained much the same as they both ran on. She could have put a spurt on and caught him up, but it felt pleasantly reassuring to have someone to follow. Because it had been raining the man had splashed mud up the back of his black Lycra leggings. Her own legs would be much the same, only looking even filthier because her leggings were bright multi-coloured in a check pattern. Anyway, it would all go in the wash this afternoon.

The man stopped to take a swig from his water bottle, looking round as he did so. He glanced at Kitty, then looked at her again more keenly, adjusting his glasses and squinting. By this time she had caught him up.

'Aren't you the lady who gave me directions last week?' he said, closing his bottle and falling into step beside her.

'Down to the canal? Yes, that was me. Did you find it OK?'

'Oh yes. And I'm glad I've seen you again, because I wanted to thank you. It was a grand route – the first part through the forest and then out into the open along the canal side. Yes, absolutely splendid.'

'I'm glad you liked it. It is lovely countryside. You're not from round here, then?'

'We moved here last summer from Birmingham, and now we live a couple of miles away from here. I must say it's a big change from city life, but it has its good points. And stunning places like this is one of them.' His voice was pleasant enough, Kitty thought. Slightly posh, but nice. You could tell that he wasn't from round here.

'Ah.' Kitty paused. This stranger seemed to be settling in beside her, running easily at her own pace. Should she just say that she preferred to run on her own? Should she just politely say 'nice talking to you' and speed up, hoping he took the hint? She did neither of these and they ran on, footfalls nearly in unison, the track through the heart of the forest easily wide enough for both of them.

Suddenly he said, 'Actually, I'm really excited. I've recently heard that I've got into the London Marathon. My first marathon! I'm going to have to do a lot of training.'

Kitty gasped and half turned towards him. 'You're not going to believe this, but so have I! When I saw you last week the acceptance letter was waiting for me at home, after being delayed for a day.' She had wondered if Doris had kept the letter for a whole day on purpose. She wouldn't put it past her.

'My letter arrived last weekend so I thought I'd better get out for a long run to kick off my training.'

They exchanged sidelong beams at each other, careful to do little more than glance because they needed to keep their attention on the rough track. They both started to talk excitedly together, then each stopped politely in deference to the other, both started talking again, and then both laughed in embarrassment.

'Most people run with a club,' said Kitty. 'I was starting to feel a bit lonely. Like I was the only person training around here on their own. I'm so glad I'm not.'

'Well, there's going to be thousands taking part in the marathon, so there's bound to be lots of people not in clubs. But I know what you mean. I'm not really one for joining clubs in general, though. How about you?'

Kitty considered. 'I wouldn't mind running with a club sometimes, but there's not one for miles and anyway I'm working most evenings and parts of the weekends, so it just not going to happen.'

He asked what job she did, and Kitty told him.

'Well I never! I wouldn't have taken you for a pub landlady. You seem... well, too young and athletic, if I may say so. I've always pictured landladies as stout bodies.'

'Not me.' Kitty said. But you haven't met my mother-in-law, she nearly added. 'I don't really think of myself as the landlady. I just take care of the kitchen and do a bit behind the bar sometimes. Sunday lunchtimes in particular. Now Rob, that's my husband, the pub is his life, pretty much. He's passionate about it.'

'Maybe we'll call in some time and have a meal.'

Kitty picked up on the 'we'. 'Is that you and your wife?'

'Yes.'

She expected him to say more, but he didn't. They turned onto the canal towpath where a patch of snowdrops nodded their heads and a couple of walkers were sauntering with their dogs.

Presently he said, 'How many miles are you doing today?'

Kitty told him she was going to do fourteen.

'Is that about right? There's half of January, February and March to build up the miles to marathon distance. Do you know, I entered for this race without a clue how to train for it. And I still don't have much idea. You simply build up the mileage week by week, I suppose?'

'I bought a book on it last year. Yes, the plan for a beginner is to stretch the weekly long run week by week - plus increasing your midweek run distance and keeping up the four shorter ones - until you get to twenty miles, do that twice and then go into the taper.'

'The taper?'

'Yes. The last two weeks you reduce the mileage right down so that you're full of energy for the race. In theory.'

'It sounds daunting. Are you nervous?'

'In some ways. I'm scared that I won't be able to do it. But I'm going to give it my best shot. I've done several half marathons, but a full marathon... that really makes you a runner.'

'Well, you sound like a very determined young woman. And organised too.'

Kitty glowed at the praise. 'Thank you. I have to be organised to fit everything in. There's Danny to look after too, my son. He's eight. A good kid, no trouble at all.'

'You're a mother too! Now that must be challenging. I often wonder how women manage to work, run a home and look after children.'

'We live in a flat over the pub,' Kitty explained. 'So it's not as if I'm actually away from Danny. And...' She hesitated. 'My mother-in-law has always helped to look after Danny.' It's true, she thought. It would be hard to manage without her. 'She lives in the cottage that adjoins the pub. What happened was that the pub used to belong for many years to her and my father-in-law, then when he died six years ago Rob took the pub over, and we moved into the upstairs flat. Anyway, I seem to be talking about myself a lot. What about you? You said you haven't lived here very long?'

He told her that they had moved to the area the previous summer and that he worked in a Finance Department. A humble clerk was how he described himself. Kitty asked him how long he had been running, and he told her that he had started about three years ago and asked the same question of her. She told him she had started when they moved into the pub, as a way of keeping fit and also getting some time on her own.

It seemed that very quickly and they were on the homeward stretch and nearly back at the car-park. They had talked for most of the run, recounting their personal histories, their running experiences, and exclaiming about the beauty of the countryside. She had never known a long run go by so quickly.

'This is me,' he said when they arrived at his car. They both flipped open their water bottles and drained what was left. Kitty had a chance to look at him over the top of her bottle. He was probably in his late forties, early fifties, she guessed.

'Thank you so much for the pleasure of your company today,' he said. 'I enjoyed the scenery, the running and learning something about you.'

Kitty picked up on his formal tone and echoed what he had said.

He flexed his limbs. 'You know, I don't feel too tired so I'll take that as a good omen for future training.' As he fumbled in his pocket for his keys and unlocked the car door he added, 'I know this is bold because you don't know me, but I'm going to come here again next Sunday to train. Do you think you might be here again too?'

She saw the red scarf lying on the passenger seat along with a thermos flask and a packet of biscuits. 'I'm planning to stick to this route for my long runs, so yes, I'll be here.'

'In that case, would it be an imposition if I asked if I could run with you again? For one thing it will give me confidence.'

Why not, thought Kitty. 'OK,' she said. 'Shall we say nine o'clock?'

His serious face lifted into a smile as he agreed. 'Oh, but I don't know your name,' he added as she turned to go.

'It's Kitty.'

'Kitty. It suits you perfectly.' He wiped his hand down the side of his leggings and held it out to her to shake hands. 'And I'm Malcolm. Adieu until next week, Kitty.'

Chapter 3

Three minutes to nine, according to Kitty's watch. She jogged on the
spot, trying to keep warm. I'll give him until five past, she thought. She
was just wondering if this might have been a bad idea when she heard
the sound of a car and the cream BMW purred into the car-park.

'Hello,' said Malcolm as he got out of the car. 'I wondered if you'd
be here.'

'I wondered about you too.'

He locked the car and stowed the keys in his inside pocket. 'But
here we both are. Shall we?' He gestured tentatively with his arm
towards the muddy path.

'Don't you want to warm up?'

'Oh.' He looked crestfallen. 'I don't usually. Should I?'

'I do. But I don't suppose it matters if you're not used to it and we
start fairly gently.' The truth was she was ready to get going and didn't
want to stand around getting chilly.

They set off through the woods and soon got up to a speed that
was comfortable for both of them.

'How was your week? Did you fit in all the runs that you wanted?'
he asked.

Kitty replied that she'd had Monday off as her rest day but that
she'd trained all the other days. Wednesday she'd run seven miles, and
the others were shorter runs.

'Goodness! That's better than me,' he said. 'I had two days off and
then only managed four miles the other days. I run lunchtimes at work,
you see, and four miles is as much as I have time for. Maybe I will have
to change to morning runs like you, or evening runs. Running in the
dark isn't very appealing...' He fell quiet.

Kitty waited for him to add more. When he didn't, she said, 'It's not

24

so bad if you stick to well-lit roads and wear a reflective tabard. And anyway, the days are getting longer each week.'

He acknowledged her with a non-committal sound and then they continued to run in silence. Kitty couldn't put her finger on it, but there seemed to be an awkwardness that wasn't there last week. She started to wish that she was on her own, like she used to be. And after she had bothered to tell Rob that she was running with Malcolm, too. She had debated this point in her mind, and of course talked to Tina about it. What else were best friends for?

'You'll never guess what, Teen,' she had said, when the two of them had their normal get-together in the week. 'You know how I normally like to run on my own? Well, last Sunday I did my long run with a man. A mysterious stranger!'

Tina's eyebrows had shot up over the top of her coffee mug. 'No! You dark horse you!' She leaned closer over kitchen table towards where Kitty sat on the other side, her long unruly hair falling forwards around her face. A pile of post and an abandoned glove lay on the table and Kitty's coffee mug, when she put it down, crunched on crumbs. Tina wasn't the most tidy of people. 'Tell, then,' she said, her eyes wide with curiosity. 'Who is he?'

Kitty drew in a deep breath and enjoyed her moment. More usually she ended up listening to Tina's scandalous stories – or imaginings, mostly. 'His name's Malcolm, he's fiftyish, I would say, drives a posh BMW and is some sort of office bod – quite senior though, I think – in a university. We just bumped into each other while I was running last Sunday and well, just sort of fell into step together. He wanted me to show him the best way.'

Tina snorted. 'Is that all he could come up with? And you fell for it?'

Kitty smiled and ran her finger round the rim of her mug. 'It's not like that. For a start, he's old enough to be my father.'

'That doesn't mean a thing.' She sat back and made herself comfortable. 'Now, I want you to tell me everything.'

So Kitty recounted everything she could think of, exactly as it happened, and answered all Tina's eager questions. They only had to break off for a few minutes to sort out the two boys who were playing upstairs in Luke's bedroom.

'Luke! We can't hear ourselves think down here!' roared Tina from the bottom of the stairs. The boys responded by charging downstairs to wheedle for more chocolate biscuits. They were in luck because Tina wanted them out of the way so that she could get the rest of Kitty's story.

'The thing is,' said Kitty after the boys had hurtled upstairs again, 'Do I tell Rob that I'm meeting up with Malcolm again this Sunday to run together? I mean, I'm not doing anything wrong and it's actually safer for me to be with Malcolm than running on my own through those lonely woods, even though he's not exactly built like a bodyguard. It all sounds like such a coincidence though, us meeting as we did, even though it's totally true.'

Tina frowned and cocked her head on one side while she considered the question seriously. Eventually she said, 'If you don't tell Rob, someone will probably spot you two running together and kindly mention it to him – you know what people are like – and that would be worse. So you're going to have to tell him something.'

So they decided that Kitty would just tell him the truth about what had happened but that she would play up – alright, exaggerate – the aspect of her feeling safer having someone with her and play down the friendly conversations that they had had.

As it happened it all went smoothly. Kitty dropped the topic into a conversation with Rob with a breezy 'oh-by-the-way' attitude in bed later, and because there had been particularly good takings over the bar that night he was in a jolly mood. She had even thought to sweeten the pill by adding that Malcolm and his wife would like to come to the pub to have a meal. New customers! That equated to pound signs in Rob's eyes. He had grunted and said he supposed it was OK. Before he could think too much about it Kitty had slid her hand down the front of his pyjamas.

*

Their run took them onto the canal towpath and skirted round a couple of over-friendly dogs. Just when Kitty thought that they weren't going to talk at all, Malcolm seemed to make an effort and broke the silence by repeating, 'How was your week?'

'Pretty standard,' replied Kitty. 'A couple of busy evenings, some quiet ones too. That's how it goes. I've had coffee with my friend and taken Danny into town to get new shoes, and we went to MacDonald's, his favourite. Oh, and I bought myself some new socks, good ones, for training. If they turn out to be OK I'll get another pair for the marathon.' She laughed. 'Quite sad, really, that the high spot of my week was buying new socks. How about you? How was your week?'

'Oh, my routine doesn't vary much. I go to work every day, get home between six and seven, eat dinner, read, maybe watch a little TV. Then on weekends there's various household jobs to catch up on, and the garden of course.'

'And what about your wife? Does she work?'

'No, Celia doesn't work. She used to like to cook and bake, but she doesn't do so much of that now.'

'And don't you see friends at all?'

He gave a short laugh. 'Since we moved here we've been a bit slow in making friends, I'm afraid.'

Kitty struggled with this concept. 'What about family? Do you have any family?'

She heard the rhythmic sound of both their footsteps slapping on the wet path while she waited for him to reply. He said 'We have a daughter, Adela. She's in her last year at university in Liverpool so we don't see her very much.' He paused. 'She keeps in touch, though, on the phone. More to her mother than me, it sometimes seems.'

The last bit seemed to be more to himself than to her, so Kitty gave up on the conversation and they lapsed again into silence. Eventually she said, 'We need to put in some extra distance today, to build up the mileage. There's a loop I'm thinking of that would add an extra mile or so, but it's up onto the ridge, and it's rather steep. There's a fantastic view from the top, though, so it's worth it. What do you think?'

'I haven't done a lot of hill running, so I suppose I should do some. And I know that we have to run further today than last week. Alright, I'll be willing to be guided by you.'

When they came to the ridge the trees closed in around them again, accentuating the darkness of the dull January morning. They had to go single file, with Kitty leading the way. She put her head down and dug

27

deep, as the running magazines she bought told her to do. She pumped her arms and legs in unison, feeling and actually enjoying the heaving of her chest as she was forced to breathe from the very bottom of her lungs. She could hear Malcolm's footsteps and increasingly laboured breathing just behind her, so she knew he was keeping up. At last they burst out through the trees onto the top of the ridge. She turned around jubilantly, ready to exclaim at the view and their triumphant climb.

At first she thought he was having a heart attack. He was bent double and strange gasping sounds were coming out of his mouth. She bent over him in dismay, asking him urgently what was wrong, and wondering whatever she was going to do. Then she realised that actually he was crying; the tears bled from his eyes and his gasping crescendoed to wracking howls that were more animal than human. He straightened up and his eyes met hers in a desperate entreaty. Instinctively she flung her arms around his heaving body and held him, making soothing sounds as if to a child, while her own breathing still laboured from the climb.

*

'I'm really sorry. I feel absolutely stupid,' he said for about the tenth time, as they sat in his car. 'Thank you so much for taking care of me like you did.' The steam generated by the cup of coffee she had poured from his Thermos flask, combined with the vapour from their bodies, had steamed up the windows, closing out the world.

'Don't worry about it,' she replied yet again. 'Have some of this hot coffee.' She passed him the cup and he took it in both hands. She studied him in concern. Straight after the outburst, she couldn't get anything out of him, apart from his abject apologies. Her innate common sense took over and she suggested that they keep going, if he could manage it, so that they wouldn't get chilled. And, of course they had to get back. He nodded and did as she suggested, head bowed and arms loose at his sides. He kept up with her, but he lumbered along as if in a dream. At first she kept shooting anxious sidelong glances at him and enquiring if he was alright, and he answered briefly that he was. After a while she could see that he could indeed cope so they finished the run in silence, the miles hanging heavily. When they got to the car he stiffly thanked her again, and after some hesitation she suggested that they both sit inside. She couldn't just leave him.

The car smelt of leather. It had obviously been recently vacuumed and the interior fittings gleamed from polish and attention. There was a pile of CDs, neatly stacked, underneath the music centre. Kitty fleetingly wondered what his taste in music was.

'Do you want to tell me what happened?' she said, after she had poured the coffee and passed it to him.

He leaned his head up against the side of the window, seeming to shrink down into himself. Here was a man who was suffering. Kitty waited.

With an effort Malcolm pulled himself more upright. 'It would have been David's birthday today. David, my son. He would have been twenty-one.'

Would have. Oh no, thought Kitty. No… 'Malcolm, I'm so sorry. What happened to him?'

Malcom fixed his gaze ahead, onto the steamed-up window. 'He had a brain haemorrhage, a year last November. It happened out of the blue, no warning. He was complaining of a bad headache one morning. We thought it was a hangover, because he'd been out with friends the night before, you know, like boys do. I went off to work as usual. Celia left him in bed and went shopping. She came home a couple of hours later, knocked on his door, but there was no reply. When she went in he was lying there, on his bed. But he wasn't asleep, he was dead.' All the passion of earlier on the ridge had left him and he recited the words in a quiet monotone.

Kitty gasped. 'Malcolm, that's… that's terrible.' She placed her hand over his. 'How *awful* for you. I can't imagine...' She trailed off, unable to find the words.

He leant his head back and continued to speak with his eyes closed. Kitty looked at him and saw how lined and tired his face was.

'He was a terrific boy. Everyone said so. A real all-rounder, you know? He did well at school – he was deputy head boy, in fact – he was all set to go to university. He was good at sport, he had lots of friends, he was good-natured. You know how some teenagers get all moody and rebellious? Not David. He had the sunniest of natures, all through his adolescence.' He gave a snort, which was probably supposed to be a laugh. 'Do you know, it was David who got me into running. We would jog a bit together on weekends - not long, just a few miles. Come on Dad, he'd say. It'll do you good after all that sitting at a desk all week long. And he was always so courteous and loving to his mother, and she doted on him. Then he died and everything fell apart.'

'That's why we moved away,' he continued. 'Celia thought it would be best to have a fresh start. So I got a job here. But it didn't help. You end up bringing it all with you, only now we don't have our old friends and neighbours to fall back on.' He turned to Kitty, and she saw the bleakness in his eyes. 'It's kind of you to listen to me like this. I don't talk to anyone about it.'

'What about your wife? Surely you talk with her about it?'

He shook his head. 'Celia and I hardly talk at all nowadays. Not about anything important anyway. It's like... it's like she's sealed herself away, behind glass. Away from me, and away from everything.'

Kitty shifted in her seat. 'I don't know what to say, Malcolm.' She squeezed his hand and felt inadequate.

He acknowledged her with a wan smile. 'The days pass. You do your normal things, and part of you gets used to it. Most days you're fine, you can cope. But another part of you thinks that nothing can ever be completely right again. Then today... I woke up and it was intolerable. God, how I miss him! How can he not be here, celebrating his twenty-first birthday? How is it *possible*? So much youth, so much promise...' He turned again to look at Kitty. 'But I am really ashamed about my outburst. After all, I hardly know you. The pain just built up inside me and, well, I couldn't control it. It was like... like a dam bursting. If I'd had your phone number, I would have phoned up and made an excuse for not coming today. But we didn't swap numbers, did we?'

'It probably did you a world of good to let it all out like that,' said Kitty. 'You seem much calmer now.'

He took a tentative sip of his coffee and she noticed that his hands were much steadier than they had been when she first gave it to him. 'Yes. Yes, actually I do feel much better. Empty and sad, but somehow... calmer.' He nodded slowly, and flexed his body gently, tentatively, as if he was waking from sleep. 'I'm sorry, where are my manners? Would you like some coffee?' He proffered the cup towards her.

'No, thanks,' she replied automatically, but then the aroma underneath her nose tempted her, and they ended up finishing the cup together and pouring another one from the flask while Malcolm talked more about David. Kitty listened without interrupting, letting the words empty out of him. He also produced half a pack of ginger biscuits, and they both discovered that they were hungry. Kitty hoped that he would excuse the crumbs that she couldn't avoid dropping in his pristine car.

Eventually he said, 'Despite what happened today, I do hope that we can run together again. I don't know if I can do this marathon, it might be too much for me. But I'd like to continue running with you. I promise you I won't go off the rails like that again.'

Kitty drew in a deep breath. 'Malcolm, listen to me. You *can* do this marathon, and you're *going* to do it. You're going to do it for David. It will be your memorial to him. We'll train together.' When he didn't reply she added, 'Say yes. I like running with you, too.'

'Yes. A memorial. That would be fitting.' She watched the slow smile lift his sad face as what she'd said sank in. 'Very fitting. Are you sure you can put up with running alongside an old man?'

She laughed, more in relief than anything. 'Not that old, I think. Now, what time is it? I should probably be getting back... *oh, my God!*' She gawped at her watch, unable to believe what she saw. 'It's five past twelve! The pub opened five minutes ago. Oh no, Rob's going to be so worried...'

She had opened the door and was half way out when Malcolm put a hand firmly on her arm. 'Get back in and I'll drive you there. It will be much quicker.'

They set off down the track to the road, Kitty wringing her hands and mumbling about how she wouldn't have time to shower and that they would be wondering what had happened to her.

It was Malcolm's turn to be the supportive one. 'I'm sure that once you explain it was my fault everything will be fine. And, if I'm not mistaken, you don't get many customers in a pub at Sunday lunchtime just after twelve o'clock, surely? It's later that they tend to come in.

31

Now, just take some deep breaths.'

Kitty did as he suggested and tried to compose herself. 'Yes, you're right.' *The Spinning Coins* came into view; it had only taken four minutes to drive from the woods. They swept into the car-park and she saw straightaway that there were already three other cars parked there and one large minibus, from which the last few stragglers were getting out and trailing into the Lounge entrance. And to cap it all, two of the local lads on their way to the Bar had turned to look half curiously at who was pulling into the car-park at such speed. Of course they spotted Kitty as she jumped out of the car and they waved cheerily to her, calling out something that she didn't quite catch.

*

'Looks like we got here just at the wrong time, didn't we,' said the woman to her husband. 'It'll take ages to just get served, let alone order our lunch. I told you we should have left home earlier.' She pulled her cardigan down and glared at the party of men in front of her, two deep at the bar.

'No use complaining now,' her husband muttered in reply. 'We'll just have to wait. Where's our Lou got to?'

'Toilet. You'd think there would be more than one person serving on a Sunday lunchtime, wouldn't you.' She turned to address Louise who had just joined them, wiping her damp hands on a tissue from her shoulder bag. 'I hope it's worth the wait.'

'It will be, Mum,' Louise said soothingly. Now then, why don't you and Dad go and get a table while I get the drinks. Oh look – that woman who was sitting on a stool at the end of the bar, she's gone to help pull some pints. That should speed things up. Go on, I'll get you your usuals.'

Louise breathed a sigh of relief when they went to sit down, with Mum complaining that it just wasn't right for customers to go and serve behind the bar. She watched as the middle-aged woman, stony faced, lined up pints of beer on the bar for the men. They seemed like a fun crowd, aged thirty to forty perhaps, a lot of banter passing back and forth between them. Clearly they had come from the minibus, and were on some sort of outing. They all looked well dressed, professional types and she wondered what the occasion might be. An office do, perhaps?

32

One or two of them were real dreamboats, And she could only wish she was here without Mum and Dad. There again, these guys were too good looking to be single.

They grabbed their pints from the bar and made off to occupy several tables. Once they had gone Louise was next in line and the landlord served her with a smile that was more like a grimace, his forehead beaded with sweat. She took the drinks and some menus over to where her parents were sitting. And yes, Mum was still scowling, armed folded and Dad was hunched on his stool, playing with a beermat. This is only once every couple of weeks, she told herself. And tonight I'm going to have a nice long bubble bath.

'Why did you bring us all the way out here, Lou?' said Mum. 'I was happy staying close to home, like we always do.'

'I told you, this is one of the places we came to on Nicola's hen night, and we all had a great meal. Good value too. And I thought a ride out into the countryside and a change would be nice for you.' Her eyes fixed on Dad. Help me out here, they said. But he was concentrating on his pint.

They made their lunch choices and Mum said she would come up to the bar with Louise to order because she wanted to ask if the Yorkshire puddings were homemade, in which case she'd have the beef; if not, she'd have the chicken. Assuming it was free range, of course.

When they sat back down Mum said to Dad, 'Well, now I've seen it all. The first woman who went behind the bar, the one who looks a bit like the Queen, well she's sat back down and now there's another woman serving, a young one, but she's all muddy – all down her calves. She's got no shoes on neither, just socks. And she looks like she's been dragged through a hedge backwards. Look!' She craned her neck to see through the men who had crowded up to the bar for their next round. 'A fine place you've brought us to, Lou.'

*

Kitty knew that she should shower first before eating her lunch but she was simply too hungry. It was twenty to three before the last customers went and since breakfast all she'd had, after running fifteen miles, was a couple of biscuits in Malcolm's car and a packet of crisps behind the bar, gobbled down when she could. There hadn't been a

33

Sunday lunchtime this busy for ages. Normally Rob would be in jubilant high spirits about the takings. But not today.

Ivy and her daughter were just finishing clearing up in the kitchen when Kitty came in, carrying the last couple of dishes, scraped clean of custard and apple pie.

'I've put your dinners out on the side,' said Ivy over her shoulder, up to elbows in suds as she scrubbed the big roasting pans. Her daughter was putting clean cutlery back into the racks. Kitty noted with the usual irritation that she performed this simple task with all the speed of an arthritic snail. Still, they always turned up, every Sunday, and you had to be grateful. 'They just need a couple of minutes in the microwave,' Ivy added.

The savoury aroma of the food percolated out of the microwave to Kitty's nose and her stomach lurched with hunger. The plates were loaded with succulent beef, roast potatoes, parsnips, Yorkshire pudding, mash, peas, carrots, cabbage and swede, with gravy in a jug on the side. A proper Sunday dinner. She took one roast potato off her plate to nibble and put the second plate in the microwave.

'Have you both had yours?' asked Kitty, one eye on the plate as it revolved hypnotically.

'Yes, we ate it while we were waiting for the last few plates to wash.'

The microwave pinged for the second time and she took both plates into the Lounge.

'Here's your dinner,' she said to Rob. 'Did Danny have his earlier with your mother?'

Rob grunted, which may or may not have been a reply. He was counting money at the till. When he had finished he joined Kitty and they ate in silence. Kitty listened to the chatter of voices in the kitchen, and the clatter of crockery and pots as they were put away, while she wolfed her dinner down. After a few minutes Ivy came in for their money, lurking by the bar in that submissive way that she always seemed to have when she was around Rob. He paid her – always cash in hand - and gave her a bit extra as a thank-you for how hard they'd both worked. Then he followed them to the door so that he could lock it behind them. Kitty listened to the slamming of the door, the turn of the key in the lock, and the decisive sound of the bolt being driven home.

Rob pulled himself a pint of bitter and banged it down on the table beside his dinner. He hadn't offered to get Kitty a drink.

'So what the fuck did you think you were doing?' he said. He stabbed at his dinner with his fork, took a mouthful and swallowed it almost without chewing. 'You were late, I didn't know where the hell you were, and you looked like something the cat had dragged in when you were behind the bar. What have you been up to?'

'I'm sorry. Just let me explain...'

'Explain!' He broke in. 'I think it's pretty clear. Geoff and Dave came into the Bar laughing and saying as how they'd seen you being dropped off in a car, a bloody great BMW, by a man, and didn't I know what my own missus is up to. Well, it's obvious what you're up to, isn't it? Stupid bastard that I am, I actually believed that you were out running. Did you shag him?' He had put down his knife and fork. His fists were clenched on the table and his face was red and ugly.

'No! It wasn't like that...'

'You expect me to believe you? You turn up nearly an hour late in some bloke's car? Do you think I'm stupid, Kitty? You've made a right fool out of me.'

'Please, Rob, I can see how it looks, but really...'

'Oh you're pathetic.' Rob shoved his half eaten dinner away, got up from the table and paced up and down the room like a caged panther.

Kitty put her hand up to her forehead. She could smell her armpit, the stale and sour sweat, like she had smelled it when she had been pulling pints behind the bar over lunchtime. 'Are you going to listen to me now?'

He turned round to her and sneered. 'What, so you can tell me about lover boy? Tell me who he is, that's all, and I'll make sure he's in no fit shape to do any more running for a long time.'

Kitty stood up and walked over to him. She tried to put her hands on his shoulders but he shook her off. 'Nothing like that, nothing sexual, happened at all, alright? He just desperately needed someone to talk to and I didn't notice the time. I know I should have done, but it truly was a one-off and it won't happen again.' She looked into his face and saw him pause briefly. But not long enough to digest what she'd said.

'You're dead right it won't happen again. Because you're not going out running with him again. Or on your own for that matter. I need you here, Kitty, helping me earn our living. *Our* living.'

She tried to keep her voice even. 'That's not fair, Rob. I slave away in that kitchen, you know I do. And please don't try to stop me running. It's pretty much my only pleasure away from this place.'

'*Away from this place?* It's that bad, is it?'

The hot dinner had revived her, giving her back her strength. She felt the blood start to pound in her temples. 'Sometimes, yes. Sometimes it feels like a prison. I know it was your dream to be a landlord of a pub just like your Dad, but it was never mine. I work hard, I support you, and I look after Danny.' The words were gathering momentum now and her voice was rising to a shout. 'And we don't even have a nice place to live, with our own front door. Just that crummy flat with the waft of stale beer always in it. I hate it here. I *hate* it.'

And there it was. They faced each other, both panting now like boxers after the first round. Kitty was the first to step back from the brink. She turned away and ran upstairs, slamming the door of the flat behind her.

Chapter 4

It would have been his seventeenth birthday – no, sixteenth because Adela was there too so it was before she went away to university. They were having a special family tea to celebrate, just the four of them, and Celia had made a birthday cake. She had carried it in from the kitchen, the candles flickering and illuminating her flushed cheeks. She was laughing and her eyes, fixed on David, were dancing with pleasure. They urged him to blow the candles out in one go, because it was good luck and he could make a wish. Had he in fact blown them all out in one go? Malcolm couldn't remember.

The shower water coursed down over Malcolm's head and body, hot and not without its own measure of comfort. He felt tired, drained, but that was hardly surprising after a fifteen mile run, which he wasn't used to, and that shameful, embarrassing outburst. And yet when he allowed himself to probe cautiously the wedge of sadness that lived inside him like indigestion he found that it was less... less what? Less sharp-edged than it had been this morning. Now it was just a dull ache.

Downstairs Celia was getting a leg of lamb out of the oven, a striped butchers' style apron covering her front. 'It will be about another fifteen minutes, so that the joint can rest,' she said.

Her cheeks were flushed today too, but that would be just from the heat of the oven. Malcolm wanted to go and take her in his arms, to say, *do you remember, Cece, do you remember his sixteenth birthday? Our boy. Our beautiful boy.* He wanted to press his cheek next to hers and feel their tears mingle quietly. But this morning, when he had started to say what day it was, she had changed the subject and he hadn't persisted. She glanced at him quizzically as he lurked in the kitchen doorway. 'I'll call you when it's ready.'

Malcolm turned to go into the living room. Then he stopped and

37

said, 'Oh, by the way, has Adela phoned?'

'Yes she phoned about eleven. We had quite a long chat.'

Malcolm felt obscurely slighted that his daughter had phoned when he was out. But she wasn't to know. Although, she usually phoned her mother in the daytime when he was at work.

'I think I'll give her a quick ring,' he said. When Celia didn't reply he added, 'Does she know what day it is?'

Celia was concentrating on mashing potatoes. 'Yes, she knows.'

Malcolm was starting to think that she wasn't in because the phone rang several times before she picked it up. 'Hello, Adela,' he said, his voice sounding falsely hearty to his own ears. When there was a baffled silence on the other end he added, 'It's me. Dad.'

'Dad... this is a surprise. I only talked to Mum this morning. Is everything alright?' Her voice was slightly breathless and he could hear the sounds of pop music playing in the background. Also there were other voices, a man and a woman it sounded like, and he had a vague picture of the flat they shared, littered with books, letters, dirty dishes, items of clothing. The picture was vague because he'd only been to visit once.

'Oh yes... yes. Everything's fine. But how are you? Are you busy? It sounds nice and lively there.'

'Yeah, everything's good. We just had pizza delivered for lunch. Well, breakfast and lunch combined, really.'

He asked her how her studies were going, trying not to sound like he was checking up on her. She told him rather guardedly that the studies were going well, a note of puzzlement in her voice. When she asked how he was, he told her about getting in to run the London Marathon, and about the training regime that he had embarked upon.

'Of course, I started to do some running with David. David was a good runner. Do you remember?'

'Yes, I remember. David was good at everything.'

'And did you remember what day it is? He would have been twenty-one today.'

He heard her breathe in sharply on the other end of the phone. In the space before she replied he heard the raucous chords of the beginning of some rock anthem. Goodness knows how loud it would be there, in Adela's flat.

'Yes Dad, I remember. I had remembered before I spoke to Mum this morning on the phone. Is that why you've called me?'

'Oh… not exactly. I mean I haven't talked to you for a while…'

She jumped in before he could finish. 'You haven't talked to me for a while because I'm not David, am I? I'm not the golden boy, I'm just the second-class daughter. When are you going to stop punishing me for being the one who's still alive, Dad?'

*

'So I couldn't just leave him. I honestly don't think I've ever seen any adult as upset as Malcolm was.' Kitty looked over at Rob from her favourite corner of the sofa where she sat with her legs curled under her. He was sprawled at his end of the sofa, the end he always had, closest to the telly. 'Have some more cake, love? And some more tea?' She sat up and hovered the knife encouragingly over the Victoria sponge on the coffee table in front of them. Soon he would have to go and get ready to open up for evening, and she knew he was tired after the busy and stressful lunchtime.

'It's good cake,' said Rob as he waded into his second slice. 'You always make good cake.'

'Thank you.' They were tiptoeing round each other, both shaken after the earlier outbursts. They had arrived at a cautious truce after Rob had allowed Kitty to tell her story. He had said little. Rob was always transparent and she could see from his face that he was busy struggling with conflicting emotions. When they had settled down on the sofa, he said that on the one hand he was proud that Kitty had been kind and caring, but on the other, she had been with another man, with all that touchy-feely stuff, even if nothing else had actually gone on.

'And I still don't understand why he suddenly goes and dumps all that stuff on you. After all, you're practically a stranger.'

Kitty considered this. 'I think perhaps that's the whole point. It's easier to talk to somebody who isn't involved, you know?' She could have added that the bond of running together, the shared repetitive rhythm of their feet, the separateness of this time from their normal daily lives, sets you up for sharing your thoughts and feelings. But instead she said, 'I don't think he intended beforehand to have a total

39

meltdown and cry like he did. He was just completely overwrought because it would have been his son's twenty-first birthday.' And his wife seems to be a total waste of space, Kitty thought.

When Rob didn't reply she added, 'He lost his *son*, Rob. You think if that happened to us. What if Danny suddenly dies like that? Can you imagine?' She scooted over from her end of the sofa and cuddled up to Rob's bulk, inserting herself under his arm. They both listened to the sound of Danny playing in his bedroom. Apparently, he was enacting a battle with his Star Wars figures. I'm going to give him an especially big hug before he goes to bed tonight, thought Kitty. Whether he likes it or not.

'Well,' said Rob, putting both his arms tight around her and kissing the top of her head, 'No giving up your day job to be some goody-goody therapist.' They both chuckled. He added, 'Do you really hate it here, Kits?'

'No, I wouldn't say I hate it. I didn't mean it.' She breathed in his particular Rob smell. 'Sometimes I do get a little bit fed up, though.' She felt him relaxing. 'And I am truly sorry that I was late today. It won't happen again. I do know that I have to play the landlord's wife role behind the bar on a Sunday lunchtime. Next week, I'll set out running earlier, so I'm sure to be back in good time.' She held her breath, dreading that he would say that he didn't want her to run anymore. But he just agreed, and she offered up a silent prayer of thankfulness. She didn't push her luck by mentioning running with Malcolm again.

*

Rob was humming a tune while he was behind the bar inspecting the rims of glasses for stubborn lipstick stains, polishing vigorously with a tea towel where necessary. The tune was something he'd heard on the radio a few times lately, when Kitty had it on upstairs. He didn't know who it was by – he never did – but it was a girl singing something about being 'all woman'. It was sultry, sexy and it had stuck in his head. He'd had a particularly good afternoon because he'd been for a short spin on his motorbike. He didn't take the bike out very often in the winter, but today he'd felt the urge to get out on it, even if it was just for for half an hour. It had whetted his appetite for a longer ride.

40

Tuesday, being Sam's day off, Rob had opened the pub up himself at six o'clock sharp. For the first hour it was usually pretty quiet, sometimes even empty, as it was tonight. He never minded, though. He pottered about behind the bar, checking and straightening here and there. It was his kingdom.

He was in the Bar when he heard the door of the Lounge open and close. He went through to the Lounge side, his smile ready. A man was shaking raindrops off his mac.

'Good evening. And a nasty one it's turned out to be. Best place to be is in here. What can I get you?' The standard patter.

'Well, actually, I've only come to return something.' The man, who Rob judged to be around fifty, frowned as he rummaged in his pockets. 'It's not in here,' he muttered. 'Now let me see, where did I put it… ah, here we are, it's in my inside pocket.'

Rob watched in amused puzzlement until the man triumphantly brandished an empty plastic water bottle from within his coat. 'I need to return this to Kitty,' he said. 'She left it in my car. I believe you must be Rob?'

Rob's mouth fell open. This was the last thing he had expected. The man was holding out his hand for Rob to shake and smiling tentatively. 'I'm Malcolm,' he said. 'I've twice been companioning Kitty on her Sunday morning runs. Or perhaps it should be, she's been companioning me.'

Rob shook his hand and stuttered out a greeting. Rarely had he felt so uncomfortable behind his own bar.

'It's a good thing that I've had to return Kitty's bottle,' Malcolm said. 'Because otherwise I might have put off coming to apologise to you for making Kitty late on Sunday. It was all my fault. I don't know if she told you what happened?' He was frowning earnestly as he blinked at Rob.

Rob shrugged, picked up a tea-towel and began polishing the glass that he had polished a few minutes previously. 'Yeah, she did say something.' He coughed. 'I'm, you know, really sorry for your loss.'

'Thank you,' said Malcolm, looking Rob in the eye. You've got to hand it to him, thought Rob, he might have gone to pieces with Kitty, but he's keeping it together now.

'I was just wondering if Kitty might be here? We didn't end making any arrangements for next Sunday.'

Rob had just started to reply when he heard Kitty's tread on the stairs. She was dressed in jeans and a sloppy sweatshirt, not having yet changed into her cooking clothes. She stopped abruptly as she saw Malcolm, and looked from one man to the other, trying to gauge the situation. Rob looking slightly flushed, but not angry. And Malcolm… well, it was the first time that she'd seen him not in his running kit, and he looked different. She barely had time to take in the collar and tie under his raincoat before his face curved into his gentle smile and he said, 'I came to return your bottle. We get used to having certain familiar things when we run, don't we, and I thought you might miss it.'

She took the battered container from him. It was true, there was a groove in the one side of it that she would caress with her thumb while she ran, comforted by the familiarity. 'Thanks for bringing it back,' she said. In the awkward pause that followed Malcolm coughed and pulled his car keys out from his pocket. Just before he could turn to go Rob said, 'Don't go without having a drink. What will it be?'

Kitty held her breath, hoping, half hoping, that he would say no. Rob's invitation had been polite and conventional, the landlord speaking.

Malcolm peeled back his cuff to peer at his watch. He looked sort of hunched; although it wasn't apparent when he ran, he had quite a stoop. It gave him an air of permanent semi-apology. He hesitated, not wanting to appear rude, perhaps. 'Well, just a half of best bitter then, thank you very much. I'm on my way home from work, but my wife doesn't serve dinner until about seven-thirty.' He took his mac off.

Rob placed the beer in front of him and waved away his offer to pay. Kitty saw Rob's eyes travelling over him, clocking the collar and tie that he was wearing underneath a navy sweater, his pale hands, the round shoulders which told of a life spent at a desk, the slight build — an advantage for running certainly, but perhaps not for much else.

Rob looked back and forth between his wife and Malcolm, who was sipping delicately at his beer. Suddenly he grinned hugely. 'It's nice to meet you, Malcolm,' he said, and slapped him on his shoulder. 'I don't go in for this running business myself, boxing and a bit of football were my sports when I had more time. But it's good to know that Kitty will have some company in those lonely woods with all this marathon training stuff. I do think you're both mad, though.'

Out of the corner of her eye Kitty saw Doris come into the Lounge and ensconce herself on her customary bar stool, craning her neck to see who the stranger was.

*

Kitty stood at her open wardrobe door, hands on hips, surveying the contents. Not that there was much to look at; most of her clothes were jeans and baggy tops, plus a couple of old shell suits, and they were all stuffed into drawers. In the wardrobe were mostly the few skirts and blouses that she wore when she had to serve behind the bar. Ah, but there was also her navy blue trouser suit. She pulled it out and laid it on the bed. That might do. And then there was that dress she had bought for a friend's wedding a couple of years ago and hardly worn since because it was a bit formal. It came to just below her knee, not quite midi length, and had a bold floral pattern. She laid it also on the bed. Yes. The trouser suit looked too severe alongside it, even though she always did prefer to wear trousers. With a dress or skirt you needed to wear tights and they made her legs feel both imprisoned and exposed at the same time.

She put the dress on and tried to look at parts of herself in the dressing table mirror. It would help if the bedroom were big enough to swing a cat in, she thought. There was hardly any space to squeeze around the double bed. She sighed and put aside the ever-present, niggling frustration that the flat was poky in order to concentrate on the immediate problem: what to wear tonight.

She could hear Rob in the bath, so she went into the bathroom to seek his opinion. 'What do you think?' she said, holding up the dress. 'Too dressy?'

Rob was reclining in the bath, a favourite pastime of his, belly protruding pallidly from the water. He had been nearly dozing and he squinted blearily at Kitty. 'God knows,' he replied. 'I'm not used to this sort of thing.'

'You're a fat lot of help,' said Kitty. 'And don't be long,' she called over her shoulder on her way out. 'We've got to go in less than half an hour. Rob groaned and submerged his head under the water, nearly causing a flood on the bathroom floor.

Kitty decided that the dress was her best bet and she went back to the bedroom to sit on the end of the bed, which also had to serve as a dressing table stool, and fished some earrings and a gold chain out of her jewellery box. She also took out her makeup bag, which contained a meagre collection of ancient tubes and pots since she hardly ever wore it. The last time had been Christmas. She scowled at herself in the mirror while she gave her short dark hair a quick comb. It sprang back up assertively despite her best efforts to tame it. Then, before she could change her mind, she slapped on foundation cream, eye-shadow, mascara and lipstick. The effect both disconcerted and pleased her. She wondered what Malcolm would think.

Last Sunday morning Kitty had waited for Malcolm, at the agreed earlier time, with some trepidation after the drama of the previous week. She needn't have worried. He was relaxed, and they had both fallen easily back into conversation, finding out about each other and generally commenting on the world around them. He had spoken a bit about David as a boy, but in a comfortable, if sad, way. He told her more about his job, his family, his home, his love of gardening and classical music. Little about his wife, though.

'We should make a schedule,' Kitty had said. Let's run fifteen miles again today, and after that we've got eight training weeks until the marathon, not counting the two weeks taper at the end. We need to work out how many miles in total to do each week, plus how many miles to do in the long run on Sundays so that we manage to fit in two twenty milers, but working up to it gradually. And where should we run the extra miles as we build up? Just extend the run we're already doing?'

Malcolm had groaned. 'I can't imagine running twenty miles,' he said. 'Let alone twenty-six. Do we only go as far as twenty miles in our training?'

'Yup,' replied Kitty. 'Once you go past twenty, that's when it all gets hard and you can hit the Wall.'

'The Wall?'

'Yes, that's what they call it. I've read all about it.' Kitty was glad to show off her knowledge. 'When your body has run out of readily

44

available glycogen stored in your liver, it has to change over to using mainly your fat reserves. The only trouble is that for some people this changeover doesn't happen easily and you end up feeling rotten. Physically whacked and emotionally confused.'

'It sounds awful. Is there anything you can do to avoid it?'

'Well, I gather it comes down to doing the right training, like we are, and having enough carbs and hydration on the day. Then it's just your particular metabolism type and mental resilience, they say. This is why we should do up to twenty miles only in training and stop before the dreaded Wall kicks in. If we depleted our glycogen now, it wouldn't have built up again in time for the marathon itself. I think.'

Malcolm didn't reply, and they ran on, their harmonised feet relentlessly gobbling up the ground in front of them. Kitty left him to ruminate on the Wall. We're both improving, she thought. We've been running for nearly two hours and we're still fresh. I couldn't have done that a month ago. She said as much to Malcolm.

'Yes,' he said absently and then, as the truth of it sank it, 'Do you know, you're right. And what's more, we should have a meeting to formulate the rest of our training schedule.' His voice gathered enthusiasm. 'We can prepare a spreadsheet.'

A meeting, thought Kitty. Me? And she wasn't even going to ask what a spreadsheet was. 'OK,' she said. 'When?'

He thought for moment. Then he said, tentatively, 'Look, why don't you and Rob come over to our house and have dinner on your night off? We can work out the grand plan after dinner.' Then he added, more to himself than to her, 'Celia used to really enjoy giving a dinner party, but we haven't entertained since we moved here. Perhaps it will take her out of herself.'

'Oh. Oh that's... that's very kind of you.' Kitty was nonplussed by the sudden offer, but it only took her a few seconds to succumb to the lure of seeing Malcolm's house and meeting the shadowy Celia in the flesh.

'We'd love to,' she said.

*

Rob lumbered into the bedroom, towel wrapped round his waist and muttering vague curses under his breath. 'Am I supposed to wear a

45

suit to this here dinner party?' he said.

Kitty shifted off her perch at the end of the bed so that he could get to the wardrobe. 'Oh hell, I don't know. I shouldn't think so. Malcolm was wearing a tie when he came here to bring my bottle back, wasn't he, so how about a nice shirt and tie, and your best trousers?'

Rob grunted and delved into his wardrobe. 'This one?' he said, holding up a cream shirt that was fairly new.

'Perfect,' said Kitty after a quick glance, having agonised too much over her own outfit to be overly concerned with his. 'I'll take Danny over to your Mum's.'

She knocked on the connecting door which went from the back corridor in the pub through to the adjoining cottage. When there was no reply she put her head round the door and called out to Doris. She heard Doris shout from upstairs for her to come in and that she'd be down in a minute.

'Let's go in the living room to wait for Granny,' she said to Danny. He immediately pulled out a book from the pile that Doris had put ready for him on the floor and started to read it. He lay on the floor on his tummy, propped up on his elbows, knees bent and feet swinging, like kids do. They had been Rob's books when he was a child, when he had lived in the flat above the pub with his Mum and Dad. How old had he been when his parents had had the cottage renovated and moved in here? She recalled Rob had said he had been a teenager. She looked around at the cosy living room. It was a homely space, with furniture and ornaments that were a bit chintzy for her taste, but nice nonetheless. On the far side of the front door – oh, what she wouldn't give for her own front door – there was the dining room and kitchen. She could picture Rob sitting at the dining table puzzling over his homework. Not that he did a lot, according to him.

She heard the creak of footsteps overhead and looked up at the ceiling. The cottage actually had three bedrooms. Two were just small single rooms at the back, but the master bedroom, at the front, was lovely. Kitty remembered the first time Rob had brought her here and she had stayed the night in one of the single rooms. She remembered the excitement when Rob had crept into her room in the middle of the night, and how they had had to put a pillow down the back of the

46

headboard to stop it banging. It was amazing, looking back, that all the giggling hadn't quenched their passion. But back then, nothing did. That was thirteen years ago, she realised with a shock. She was twenty and Rob was twenty-two. Where had it all gone?

She was so caught up in her reverie that she jumped when Doris came into the room, wearing her dressing gown and with her hair in a towel turban.

'I was in the bath,' she said. 'I wasn't expecting you just yet.'

Kitty stood up. 'Oh I'm sorry. I thought I'd said half past six.'

Doris waved her apology away. 'It doesn't matter. A bit more time to see my boy. It's been a while since you've slept in Granny's cottage, hasn't it.' Danny jumped up and sat by her on the sofa with his book, eager to show her Dan Dare's exploits.

'It's a school day tomorrow, Danny, so you can't be too late in bed, remember,' said Kitty. Neither Danny nor Doris said anything and Kitty decided not to push it. She had to admit that it was handy to have Doris to babysit.

Doris glanced up at Kitty and then looked again. Kitty felt every inch of her being scrutinised and she braced herself.

'You look nice. You've done yourself up a treat.' Kitty blinked back her surprise at the compliment. But it was reassuring and it did her confidence a world of good to pass the Doris test.

'You're going out to some new friends' house for dinner, Rob told me. Anyone I know?'

'Not really,' said Kitty vaguely. 'Goodness, is that the time? Come and kiss me goodnight, Danny. And now I've really got to get going.'

*

'This is it,' said Kitty, 'That's Malcolm's car on the drive. He said we could pull up behind it.' It was a detached house with a lamp over the front door that glowed softly, exuding a subtle welcome. In the darkness a neat herbaceous border and square lawn were just visible. Kitty clutched the bottle of wine on her lap. It was the best that they had in the pub, but should they have bought a better one? The smugness of the house had unnerved her.

Rob, on the other hand, now seemed resigned to his fate and was prepared to overlook that right now he could have been lying on the sofa digesting his steak-and-kidney pie while he caught up on some of his favourite TV programmes. 'Ready, then?' he said, jauntily. Then he whispered in her ear, 'And remember I'm doing this for you. I shall expect payment.'

They heard the sound of muffled voices within the house as they stood on the doorstep, their smiles ready to spread on their faces. The door swung open.

'Hello! I hope we're not late!'

'Not at all, do come in,' said Malcolm. He was dressed in a sweater and slacks. No tie. He called towards the kitchen, 'Celia, our guests are here.'

Then there was a flurry in the hallway as they fumbled to hand over their coats and present the bottle of wine. Celia appeared from the kitchen and stood by her husband, matching her welcome smile to his. She shook hands with them both while Malcolm did the introductions. Kitty tried to get a good look at Celia without actually staring. The thought came into her head: why is it that people never look like you expect them to look? Her picture of Celia was someone dowdy and sour-faced. But the woman who was looking at her – and probably appraising her in the same way, thought Kitty with a twinge of discomfort – was the picture of elegance in her plain blue skirt, silky blouse and obviously expensive court shoes. Her fine fair hair drifted in effortless ripples to graze her shoulders, and she smelled of something expensive. And – the biggest surprise – she was plump. Not exactly really fat, but certainly very ample.

Kitty was digesting this as they were shown into the living room and settled onto the sofa. Rob was asking Malcolm something about his car. Boring, but at least they were talking. Her eyes had swivelled round the room and managed to take in its neatness and quiet good taste before she had to respond to Celia's question about what she wanted to drink. Dry sherry, medium sherry and gin and tonic were offered.

God, she sounds as posh as she looks, thought Kitty. She asked for a gin and tonic, and Rob had an orange juice because he was driving. Kitty gulped at the drink when Celia handed it to her, the ice cubes clinking and the fizz tickling her nose. She began to relax as the alcohol hit her. Really, they were being made very welcome. And the house was amazing. She didn't think she'd ever been in such a lovely house. The carpet was a deep pile type, predominantly forest green with lighter green swirls, making her want to kick her shoes off and curl her toes into it. The sofa with its fat cushions seemed to envelop you in a hug and the coffee table in front of them gleamed with polish. But then, she had been brought up in a council house so almost anywhere was going to be better than that.

Suddenly her drink was gone. She realised she had drunk it very quickly, and Celia hadn't been stingy with the gin. When Celia said that dinner was ready and would they like to come through to the dining room, the world swam pleasantly as she got up. The table was set ready: a thick white table cloth, wine glasses, gleaming cutlery, prawn cocktails and a plate of brown bread and butter cut into neat triangles made an impressive picture, and Kitty slid wordlessly into her chair in awe. There were also crisp linen napkins – not paper serviettes – inserted into rings on each matching side plate. Kitty tried to catch Rob's eye to remind him to put his napkin on his lap, but he was talking to Malcolm so she gave up and just drank the wine that had been poured, ate her food with gusto and joined in the conversation that was flowing comfortably, somewhat to Kitty's surprise. They touched on the marathon, the beauty of the surrounding area, *The Spinning Coins* and pubs in general. Celia asked Kitty about her role in the pub, and how she ran her kitchen. It amused Kitty that Celia seemed to think that she had a team of well-trained assistants in there. There wouldn't be room, for a start.

Kitty realised that the way they were being drawn into the exchange and put at ease was something that Malcolm and Celia were used to doing. They weren't making a special effort just for them; this was what sophisticated middle-class people did. But it was all lovely and Kitty was having the time of her life. Even Rob seemed glad to relax and chat as he drank a glass of red wine with his beef bourguignon followed by home-made apple pie and cream.

*

'That was a fantastic meal,' said Rob. 'I'm stuffed. He patted his stomach. You can't beat proper home cooking, I say.'

Celia thanked him and said it was nothing, but he thought she was

49

pleased. She was sitting on the edge of an armchair in the living room, pouring coffee from a pot into four matching cups with saucers. The sound of Malcolm and Kitty's voices, and sometimes Kitty's laughter, could be heard coming from the study across the hall, to where they had escaped after dinner to put their heads together about their plan. Their grand training plan. Well, there doesn't seem to be any harm in the man, thought Rob. And it's keeping Kitty happy. Celia excused herself to take two cups of coffee to the study. Rob sat back and sneakily undid his belt an extra notch. The evening hasn't turned out too bad at all, he thought, although I could do without having to sit and make small talk to this Celia now. Still, I make small talk often enough to people I don't know when I'm behind the bar. But not usually to a lady. And she is a lady alright.

'How are they getting on?' he asked when Celia came back.

'I didn't enquire. They seem very engrossed.' She sat back in the chair and crossed her legs. 'Training to run the marathon seems to be good for Malcolm. It's given him some focus.'

'But rather them than us, eh?' said Rob. She responded with a slight smile. Rob ran his finger round the inside of his collar, wondering if he could surreptitiously undo his top button.

'Do take your tie off if you would be more comfortable,' Celia said.

At first Rob was embarrassed that she'd noticed his discomfort, then he thought, why not, and complied with a sigh of relief when his neck was at last unconstrained. They sipped their coffee. Rob glanced around the room for inspiration. He spotted framed photos on the sideboard alongside him. One was a family group, Celia and Malcolm with two children who looked to be around twelve to fourteen. She had seen him looking at it and now he had to say something. He coughed. 'I was sorry to hear about what happened to your son.' She thanked him, with great dignity, he thought.

'That picture was taken on holiday in France,' she said. 'We used to have a holiday home there.'

'I've never been to France,' he replied and an awkward silence followed. How long was this training plan going to take, he wondered. 'It's a good spot you've got here,' he blurted out. 'I came past earlier today when I was out on my motorbike, and I happened to notice that it's a good spot here.' He nodded earnestly. It was part true anyway. This part of the road was straight and it had enabled him to overtake the tractor that he had been following for a while.

To his surprise her face lit up. 'You have a motorbike? My father was a great motorcycling enthusiast. He had a Triumph Bonneville. When I was a small child my mother and I would ride in the sidecar. Then when I was older I would sometimes ride pillion with him. He was a member of the local motorcycling club and I used to go to events with him. I probably have some old photographs somewhere.'

'My motorbike belonged to my Dad. It was his pride and joy. I think of him every time I ride it.'

She smiled. 'It seems we have something in common. We both have fathers who were passionate about motor cycles.'

I would never have put this posh woman down as someone who used to go on the back of a bike, thought Rob. It's true what they say. There's nowt queer as folk.

Chapter 5

'Honestly, Tina, it was probably the nicest house I've ever been in. There was even this thing in the downstairs toilet that squirts out a perfume every so often. I would have loved to see what the kitchen and the bedrooms were like.'

'I'm sure Malcolm would have shown you the bedroom if you'd asked him,' replied Tina.

Kitty decided to ignore this. She shivered and burrowed her hands deep into the pockets of her parka. There was a sharp wind this morning and it was cold waiting at the bus stop for the school bus. Still, it was chasing away the remnants of her hangover. She had woken up with a thick head and a bad taste in her mouth, and had groped her way into her running kit then stumbled to the kitchen to put the kettle on and get Danny's breakfast. One mug of Nescafe and she was starting to feel better, so she could present herself more or less respectably to Rob with his cup of tea in bed and she could appear normal to Doris and Maisie when she went downstairs. Yes, there they were again, sat enjoying a cup of tea with the cleaning half done. That was a battle she wasn't going to win so nowadays she simply ignored it. She had wondered when she took Rob his tea if he would comment on her giggly state in the car on the way home last night, but all he said was that he had surprised himself by enjoying the evening and he hoped that they could return the hospitality by having Malcolm and Celia for a meal in the pub sometime, on the house. He had said as much to them last night while they said their goodnights on the doorstep, Kitty at his side grinning inanely and clutching her print-out of their agreed training plan.

After seeing Danny off on the bus a brisk five mile run in the sharp winter morning left her no room to feel sorry for herself. A hot shower, a bacon sandwich, more coffee, and then she was more than ready for her customary Tuesday trip to town with Tina for shopping, lunch and gossip.

The bus to town wheezed to a halt alongside them and they climbed aboard, as eager as truanting schoolgirls.

'You should have seen his home computer too, all set up on a desk in his study. It was an Amstrad.' Kitty pronounced the word carefully. 'And he actually had a printing machine connected up to the computer so that we could get a sheet of paper with what was on the computer screen. So we were able to sort out the whole training plan, week by week, then he put it on this computer table thingy – I think it was a spreadsheet - and then he transferred it to the paper. Just like that! We ought to have some sort of computer for Danny when he gets a bit older. The trouble is neither Rob nor I know a thing about them.'

'Me neither. But never mind about that,' said Tina. 'What was the food like? What was *she* like? You said he made her sound like the Wicked Witch of the East.'

'The food was pure heaven, and there was loads to drink. I haven't had that much to drink for ages. And as for Celia... she really wasn't what I had expected. She's about forty-five, I would say, very well preserved even though she was overweight. And her clothes were smart, expensive-looking and...and well-cut, you know?'

'No, not really. I don't exactly go in for well-cut designer jeans and jackets, do I?' Tina gestured to her usual garb of old jeans, sweatshirt and boots. 'But go on.'

'Well, she made us really welcome in a cool sort of way. And her voice! She had this really posh voice. Well no, not posh exactly... I know, *cultured*. That's it, she was cultured.' Kitty sat back, satisfied that she had put her finger on it.

'Ooh, la-di-da. Get you, mixing with cultured people. What about Malcolm, is he cultured too, taking you into his study and all that?' Tina was lapping it all up.

'Not exactly. No, I wouldn't say so. I'd describe him more as... more as educated, perhaps.' Kitty stopped abruptly and turned to look out of the window. 'There's lots of traffic today,' she said. She didn't want Tina giving Malcolm a label. He was a nice, kind man who shared

53

her love of running. That's all.

*

It had been a steady lunchtime. They had done six meals, which wasn't at all bad for a Tuesday. It was a sunny day, but Rob had discovered that that could play either for or against you. It might tempt people to come out for a drive and a meal, but equally they might decide to go for a walk instead and pop into a café.

Quarter to two. Rob was whistling a tune as he collected the last two plates and glasses from the table in the Lounge. That would be it now. He popped to the kitchen to tell Ivy that she could start finishing up now.

The winter sun was flooding in low through the windows when he went back into the Lounge, blinding him briefly, so that at first he couldn't make out the figure standing there. The rustle of movement caught his attention and he shielded his eyes with his hands, and squinted. His impression was of a halo of silvery sunshine glinting on fair hair. Then a woman stepped forward out of the sun into the shade and he could see her properly.

He blinked, his eyes still affected by the light. She was wearing a light coloured jacket with a reddish silky scarf at her neck, gloves to match, and she carried one of those old fashioned wicker baskets like you would see in an Agatha Christie film. 'Well. This is a surprise,' was all he could say.

Celia put her basket down on one of the tables, peeled off her leather gloves and laid them in it. 'I was just passing,' she said. 'Yesterday I managed to find some pictures of my father with his motorcycle, and I thought you might like to see them.' She pulled a big brown envelope out from the basket as she sat down. 'Do you have time?'

Rob said that he did have time, and asked what she wanted to drink. As he was pouring her white wine she picked up a menu. 'I'm not too late to order lunch, am I? Is there anything that you recommend?'

Rob told her that Kitty's fish pie was always a favourite and she accepted his recommendation. He left her sipping her wine while he took the order to the kitchen.

Ivy was stood at the sink washing the pots.

'One more for you, Ivy. A fish pie with salad not veg, please.'

Ivy regarded him over her shoulder, resting her sudsy arms on the edge of the sink. 'But you said we were finished. I've put everything away now,' she said.

'Well, you can get a portion of fish pie out of the freezer, can't you, and knock up a bit of salad.'

Ivy sighed and dried her hands slowly. Her face was mute with all the resentment she didn't dare to express. He wished that Kitty were here. She might not have been best pleased about having to do a late meal, but after an initial grumble she would have got on with it quickly and efficiently, like she always did. And she would probably have liked to see Celia again. They had seemed to get on well enough the other night. At least, as well as two women can when one is classy and refined and the other is… well, Kit had made a big effort, but he knew her natural self was happiest in jeans or a tracksuit.

'It'll be just a few minutes,' said Rob to Celia as he put her knife, fork and napkin on the table. She had already got the photos out. 'Wow,' he said as she passed him a grainy black and white photo of a man sitting on a motorcycle, his helmet dangling from one hand and his body encased in a bulky suit and boots. Other pictures showed bikes posed in front of a clubhouse, or riders circling on a track. Some of the photos went back to the 1950s, Celia told him. Then she passed him another one of the man on his motorcycle – the same man as in the first picture - with a small child standing next to him, a little girl aged about seven or eight, her long blonde plaits tied off with ribbons at the ends and neat little white socks. Both she and the man had the same shape of face and smile.

'I don't need to ask who that is,' said Rob.

Celia ran her finger over the picture as if she wanted to reach into it. The light caught the pale pink polish on her nail. 'I wasn't always fat like I am now,' she said.

'Fat? You're not fat. You're nicely rounded.' Rob was always genuinely puzzled when women of Celia's size and shape thought they were fat.

She smiled and inclined her head. 'You're very kind. Well, I don't suppose I shall ever be as slim and athletic as Kitty, for instance.' She

55

craned her head to look over his shoulder. 'Is she in the kitchen today?'

'No, not today. On Tuesdays she often goes out with her friend. An excuse for a good gossip session from what I can gather. She'll be sorry she missed you.'

'And I her… Ah, here comes the famous fish pie. Oh, this looks wonderful.' She nodded her gracious thanks at Ivy, who managed a tight smile in return.

Rob left her to eat her food, while he made himself busy washing the last of the glasses behind the bar. He kept sneaking surreptitious glances at her. She ate delicately, like you might expect. She chewed each mouthful thoroughly, sipping at her wine now and again. No gulping and wolfing it down. Those pictures: they had quite taken him back to his own boyhood and his own Dad. Not as long ago as Celia's pictures, of course; he was a child of the sixties. He remembered sitting astride the front of the bike while Dad rode him round the car-park. He would only have been what, four, five? But he could see it quite clearly in his mind's eye. If Celia had time after she had eaten her lunch, he would tell her about it.

*

Malcolm looked at his watch and saw that it was already five past eight. Kitty had never been late before. He tapped his fingers on the steering wheel of his car and peered into the woods. The visibility was poor today, but he would surely see her approaching. He got out of the car so that he would have a better view. Immediately the cold rain sliced down on him and he pulled up his hood. He jogged on the spot and did a few half-hearted leg stretches to keep warm. Surely she was coming? The rain wouldn't have put her off, would it? Was it anything about the evening at his house last Monday? For him it had been splendid. Celia had been something like her old self back in the days when they used to entertain quite frequently – friendly, welcoming, relaxed, efficient. The epitome of a good hostess. In fact, after they had gone home he had enquired anxiously if she had had a pleasant evening – it could all have been a polite front – and he thought it was genuine when she said she had enjoyed it. It was a surprise to him that she had found Kitty and Rob 'interesting' because, although it made him uncomfortable to admit it, they weren't the sort of people they usually mixed with. After they had gone home, he and Celia had stood together in the kitchen chatting about them, him passing her the dirty crockery and cutlery, she stacking them in neat rows in the dishwasher. It was the most intimacy that they had had for weeks.

He decided to set off down the footpath towards the pub. He was just reflecting that Kitty actually had to go an extra half mile each way along this path to get to the car-park, when he saw her coming. She waved when she spotted him.

'Sorry I'm late,' she panted. She had obviously run quite fast along the path. 'Slight crisis in the kitchen. Nothing to bore you with.'

'I'm pleased you're here at all. It must be such a rush for you, with all you have to do.' They settled into their pace, side by side.

'Worth it,' said Kitty, her breathing settling back down. 'But what a foul day! This is the worst weather we've had yet for our long run. We've been lucky so far.'

With his hood up, Malcolm had to strain to hear her so he pushed it back and allowed the rain to fall softly onto his scalp and run down his face. It wasn't so bad. 'And only another nine weeks to go after this. You'll notice I've been consulting our training plan. I have one on my desk at home in the study and another one on my notice board at work. Some of my colleagues have commented on it.' He was indeed gaining some kudos in the office with his growing athletic prowess. Or was it mockery? Or simply disbelief?

'It's a sensible plan,' said Kitty. 'We should be able to achieve it.'

'As long as we don't come down with any bad colds or injuries.'

Kitty replied promptly, 'Don't even think it. If you don't tempt fate, it won't happen.'

'You don't really believe that, do you?'

'Oh yes I do. Thinking positive is always best. You can actually attract good luck, you know, by thinking positive.'

How uncomplicated she is, he thought. And how young. Life has not yet tarnished her. But even if I had thought positively, David would still have died. No. Don't go there again.

'I do so greatly enjoy our time together, you know,' he said. 'Both the physical act of running and our conversations. If it is possible to attract good luck, then I must have been extra lucky that day I asked you how to get down to the canal. What a marvellous coincidence.'

'There you are, you see. That was an example of good luck in action. There's no such thing as coincidence. It's all syn... synco... Oh, what is it?'

'Do you mean synchronicity?'

'Yes that's it. Synchronicity.'

How wonderful to have her simple view of life, Malcolm thought. She is like a refreshing spring of water. He was considering how to reply when she said, 'Anyway, I want to say what a fab time we both had last Monday, and to say thank you. I guess I should have phoned before and said, but somehow the week seems to have been particularly busy.'

'You're most welcome. Celia and I had a lovely evening too.'

'And... and I just wanted to say that I'm sorry that I got a bit drunk.' Her words came out in a rush.

He turned sideways in surprise to look at her and saw that she was indeed shamefaced. 'You weren't particularly drunk at all. You've got nothing to reproach yourself with.'

'Are you sure? That's kind of you.' He heard the relief in her voice.

She continued, 'You see, I felt a bit nervous and overwhelmed - meeting Celia, being in an unfamiliar place, and all that. And your house is... well, I've never been anywhere like it. I'd do anything to live somewhere like that.'

'Really?' He was perplexed, trying to imagine what her life was like, living above a pub. 'What was your parents' house like?' he asked.

Kitty snorted. 'Well, not like yours, that's for sure. We lived in a council house. Then my Dad cleared off when I was eight. After that, Mum just lost it and took to the bottle. I got away as soon as I could when I was sixteen and left school. Thank goodness I met Rob.'

Malcolm was shocked at how cheerfully she came out with this, as if it were normal. For some people, perhaps it was. What a sheltered and predictable life I have led, he thought. Straight to university after school, a sensible but boring job, meeting and marrying Celia, two children. The years have slipped neatly by. This marathon is the nearest I've ever got to doing something adventurous.

'Is your life better now?' he asked.

'Oh there's no comparison. We have Danny, and we have a secure living. It's not perfect of course. One day I'd love to have my own house with my own front door. But it's good enough.'

'Have you ever worked anywhere else besides your own pub?'

'I worked in a bakery when I left school. Then I worked in a couple of shops. When Rob took over the pub and we moved here, the only thing I could do, really, was to work with him. Then we had Danny, of course. The poor little thing has never known anything else but life in a pub. But then, it didn't do Rob any harm.'

'It sounds quite a tough life compared to mine,' he said. 'All I've ever done is work in an office. I've never got my hands dirty, apart from gardening, in my life.'

'Mmm.' He wasn't sure if the sound she made was agreement or doubt. Then after a pause she followed it with, 'I've often wondered about working in an office. So many people work in an office. But I don't understand what all these people actually really *do*? I mean, policemen, teachers, factory workers, doctors; I can understand that they either make something or do something. But people who sit behind desks all day... how many pieces of paper can you actually keep pushing around?'

Malcolm opened his mouth to explain what his job in The Finance Department entailed on a day-to-day basis, the accounting, the budget calculations, the bookkeeping, the meetings and committees, but then he stopped. What exactly *do* I do that is vitally important, he thought. She's right. I don't save lives, I don't make anything with my hands, I don't directly serve society. He felt crushed by the weight of his own uselessness.

The rain was still falling steadily. She was waiting for him to answer. He pulled himself together with an effort. 'I can see how it seems that way,' he said, injecting his tone with lightness. 'And I agree that there is a certain amount of redundant administrative work. For my own part, I could explain some of the aspects of my job but, to be honest, there's a lot more interesting things that we can talk about.' Suddenly he had an idea. 'If you like, one day you could come to my office and see for yourself.'

She hesitated. 'It's a kind offer, but I'd feel a bit nervous.'

He was already regretting his impulse, imagining how the gaggle round the water fountain would view Kitty, so he wasn't sorry that she hadn't said yes straight out. 'We can see later on,' he said. 'And now let's talk about something else.'

*

Rob fumbled with the lock to the shed. There; he'd got the padlock undone and he swung the doors open. And there she was, waiting, silently veiled. He pulled the tarpaulin off and felt a mixed surge of pride coupled with pleasurable anticipation as the bike emerged. Going on a quarter of a century old and still in good nick. Mind, he had looked after her, always following up on servicing and maintenance, and giving her a good clean whenever he had been out for a ride. Which hadn't been often enough lately.

He put his helmet down on the floor while he wheeled the machine out to survey it. He had checked the tyres and petrol yesterday, so he was all ready to go.

'Going out for a ride, are you?'

'Hello Ma, I didn't hear you. Still looking good, isn't she. Just like you.'

She came up to stand alongside him.

'Flattery will get you nowhere, my lad,' she said, but he knew she was pleased.

Rob zipped up his leather jacket and picked up his helmet. 'Seeing as it's a nice day I thought I'd go for a jaunt out into the countryside.'

She raised her eyebrows in surprise. 'It won't be much of a ride if you're going to be back in time to open up at eleven-thirty.'

'Aha,' he said. 'Sam's been asking to have some overtime because he's a bit short lately, so he's going to do the lunchtime session.'

Doris didn't comment. Sometimes with Ma you never knew if she approved or not. 'And Kitty? Is she off on one of her Tuesday jaunts with that Tina?'

'Yes, she always looks forward to that.' He knew he didn't really have to explain himself, but still he added, 'She knows I'm taking the bike out though. She's fine with it.' He stood awkwardly, waiting to be dismissed.

Doris sniffed. 'If you say so. Well, ride carefully. That's what I

60

always used to say to your father.'

*

The roads were nice and dry, so Rob stepped up the power as he headed out of the village. He felt the throb of the engine underneath him and heard its low throaty purr, and his body surrendered to the machine. With every mile a bubbling lightness welled up inside him. Oh, it had been too long since he'd had a proper ride! And here was the long stretch where he could start to open her up. Should he do that, or should he slow down and look for the house?

He pulled onto the drive and brought the bike to a halt on the gravel. Probably nobody would be in, anyway. He peeled off his clumsy gauntlets to ring the doorbell. First of all, silence. He was about to turn to go when he heard a door opening in the back of the house.

She was wearing an overall and carrying one yellow rubber glove, like a dying flower, in her other gloved hand. For a second her eyes held no recognition. Rob hastily removed his helmet and visor.

'Oh,' she said. 'Hello.'

'I was just passing,' said Rob. I thought you might like to see my motorbike. You know, since you showed me your pictures. I didn't know whether or not you'd be in. But if you're busy it doesn't matter.' He trailed off and clenched his gauntlets in his hand.

Celia's eyes went past him to the where the bike was propped on its stand. 'Ah, another old Triumph. It's a beauty. I'll just pop a coat on and you can show me properly.'

He stood with bashful pride while she exclaimed over the bike, running her hand over the curve of the seat. She told him that it took her back so vividly to her youth, when her father used to ride. 'Have you got time for a cup of coffee?' she asked.

He sat at her kitchen table while she boiled the kettle and put biscuits on a plate. Then she sat opposite him, smiling dreamily while she reminisced about her past.

'Does your bike have a name?' she asked. Daddy used to call his 'Boagenes.' It means 'son of thunder'. It certainly used to emit a loud roar.'

Rob shook his head. 'Maybe I should give it one. I always think of the bike as a she, though.'

'Isn't that ships?'

'Is it? Well then, she's my two-wheeled ship.'

Celia laughed, more than his feeble joke deserved, he felt.

'Does Kitty ride pillion with you sometimes?'

'She hasn't for a long time. And then it was only the odd time. She said she never liked wearing the helmet – it made her feel like her head was being crushed. When we were courting I had a car and that was more... convenient.' He moved on swiftly. 'You said the other night that you used to ride pillion with your father sometimes?'

'Oh yes. I loved it. From when I was about fourteen to eighteen I would go out with him some weekends, when the weather was fine. Sometimes he would take me along with him to the club, or we would just go for a spin on a Sunday afternoon. There was a little café that we would stop at and have tea and scones. I haven't thought about it for years.' She stirred her coffee slowly.

'Did your mother ever go?'

'Mummy? Oh no. No.' She frowned slightly and looked down into the circling liquid in her cup. 'It wasn't her thing at all. She leaned over the table towards Rob. 'So you see, I had him all to myself when we went out together on those afternoons.' Then she sat back, head on one side and examined him with her eyes. 'Do you know, you look a bit like him. The same build, the same expression sometimes.'

Rob shuffled in his seat. The close scrutiny had made him feel uncomfortable. 'Or maybe it's just the leathers, bringing it all back.'

She dropped her eyes and shrugged. 'Maybe. Anyway, where are you going to ride to today?'

He drained the last of his coffee. 'I don't really know. Sam, that's my barman, is taking the lunchtime shift at the pub today and Kitty has gone out with her friend so I'm free as a bird for a few hours. I thought I might ride up into the hills where it's quiet.'

She turned her head and gazed out of the window. 'Will you excuse me a minute,' she said.

The kitchen clock ticked sedately. Rob could hear her now and again moving around upstairs. He pushed his chair back and looked around the room, taking in nothing. He folded his arms and then unfolded them and consulted his watch. She'd been gone for several minutes now.

He heard her tread on the stairs again, accompanied by a semi-familiar creaking, swishing sound with each step. Before he could believe what the sound was, she was back in the kitchen.

'I found them,' she said. She was wearing a black leather jacket and trousers, a white silk scarf around her neck and a red helmet under her arm. The contrast between her silky hair and soft pale features with the motorbike leathers, releasing a faintly familiar and not unpleasant smell of years of use, took his breath away.

'These were Daddy's,' she said. 'But the helmet was my own.' She fitted the helmet and zipped up the jacket, covering over, yet mysteriously enhancing, her femininity.

*

Afterwards Rob could hardly believe what had happened. He had thought only to call in and show her his bike. The last thing in the world he thought would happen was that she would climb easily on behind him and settle herself deep into the seat. As the wheels swept the miles under them he felt her gloved hands resting lightly on his waist and her body leaning in unison with his around the bends. They travelled up into open country, over moorland. In these high places he was conscious of her and yet not so, because she blended with him and the bike so well.

They dropped down into a valley, stopped at a roadside café and sat outside for a sandwich and a hot drink, cold hands wrapped around their mugs. What had they talked about? He couldn't properly remember, but it was centred around motorbikes, open countryside, freedom and rides they had enjoyed. She had been laughing, buffed by fresh air and lit up with a nostalgic pleasure she had thought never to experience again. Then he dropped her back at her house and she thanked him gravely. He looked over his shoulder to see her waving to him from the front step, her fair hair once more exposed.

Back at home he duly gave the bike a once over with a cloth and put it away in the shed. Kitty was already back. She was sitting with Danny on the sofa, both of them watching cartoons. Her feet were up on the coffee table and they were sharing a packet of crisps.

'Hello,' she said. 'Did you have a good ride? Doris said that you actually did go. I thought you were a bit unsure this morning.'

He kissed her on the top of her head and ruffled Danny's hair. 'It was great. I'd forgotten how much I enjoy a good run out on the bike.'

Her eyes were hypnotised by the gambolling shapes on the screen. She tipped her head back and shook the last of the crisps into her mouth. She said through the crumbs, 'You should do it more often, then.'

'Yes,' he said. 'I think I will.'

Chapter 6

'Good day to you, Madam, Sir,' said the Major to Kitty and Rob as he removed his overcoat and scarf and hung them on the coat-stand by the door. 'Chilly morning, or should I say afternoon now?' He rubbed his hands briskly and looked at the clock over the mantlepiece. 'Am I your first customer?'

'Yes, you've beaten the rush,' said Rob, pulling him his pint.

Kitty said her hello to him while she was making herself a big glass of orange squash and chewing a mouthful of peanuts from the bowl on the bar.

The Major tut-tutted and wagged a finger at her. 'You'll spoil your lunch, you know. Not to mention spoiling that trim little figure of yours.' His eyes travelled down her.

Kitty took a long draft of squash. 'This morning I've run seventeen miles and, even after the three pieces of doorstep toast I ate afterwards, I'm still ravenous.'

Even though she spoke lightly, Rob was aware of her irritation.

'Seventeen miles, eh? I used to do that with a twenty pound pack on my back, back in my young days.'

'Just last year, then,' said Rob quickly, before Kitty could reply.

But the Major wasn't listening. Ma had come in and he practically stood to attention to greet her. She inclined her head to return the greeting, and he lightly held her elbow to assist her onto the bar stool.

Rob glanced into the Bar: still empty. Now was his chance. After Kitty came back from her run she had been either in the shower or getting dressed and eating her toast at the same time while he was playing a game with Danny, so there had been no opportunity to talk to her.

'So,' he said to her, 'Good run this morning, was it?'

She nodded enthusiastically. 'Great. I'm not feeling tired at all.' Her hair was looking darker than usual because it was still damp, and lay in little points on the back of her neck.

'Good, good.' He pushed the bottles of orange juice into a straight line on the shelf where they were stored. 'And Malcolm? How did he do today?'

'Fine, I think. We seem to be pacing it OK. Eight minute miles is just right for both of us.'

'And did you have a nice chat like you usually do? Did he have anything special to say?' He pulled out a new pack of beermats from a cupboard underneath the bar. 'Oh, and how's Celia, by the way?' he added as he fumbled to open the pack.

Kitty was busy chomping another mouthful of peanuts. 'Oh, we talked about all sorts of things. Let's see, did he mention Celia?' Rob waited. She was frowning as she chewed as if puzzling to remember. 'I think he just said that she was OK.' Then she added, 'Rob, what are you doing? We already have a new pack of beermats open here.'

'Have we? God, I'm going senile.' He grinned at her and squeezed her arm. 'Good job I've got you to keep me on the straight and narrow, love.'

*

Rob pulled away from the pub on the motorbike, hardly able to believe his luck that the weather was dry again. He had remarked as much to Kitty that morning and had said that since she was doing her regular Tuesday trip out with Tina, he would have a ride out on his bike again. Sam was happy to do the lunchtime session. Kitty had nodded vaguely, busy as she was with getting Danny ready for school.

Whatever happens it will be nice, he told himself as he pulled his helmet visor down. She might not be home, or the novelty might have worn off and she won't want to come out again. In that case I'll just enjoy the ride on my own. In fact that might be better.

Two hours later they were sitting outside the same café as last week, with their sandwiches and steaming mugs of tea.

'Tell me about yourself,' Celia said. 'How did you come to be the landlord of a country pub?'

'I was born there,' he told her, 'I was actually brought up in *The*

66

Spinning Coins. My Dad kept it for years. When I left school I went to work as an apprentice carpenter and I would help out a bit on weekends. Then when Dad died I took over.' He took a slow sip of his tea. 'I'd always dreamt of following in my Dad's footsteps, you know, working in the pub trade and eventually having my own pub, but I wouldn't have wanted it to happen like that. He had a heart attack, you see.' He gazed out over the valley while he allowed the pictures in his mind to fade. 'I think he would have been proud of me, though. I've built the place up a lot, and we're known all around for good beer, good food and a good welcome.'

'How fascinating,' said Celia. Rob looked at her in some surprise. He wasn't used to having his life called 'fascinating.' But she was looking at him intently and it didn't seem like she was being sarcastic. Or over-polite. 'It seems like the business is a very successful one,' she added.

'We do our best,' said Rob, trying to be modest. 'My dream is to be in The Good Pub Guide. Or at least in the Lucky Dip section of it anyway.' He sat back and imagined, as he often did, how that would feel. 'Yes, I'd be a very happy man if that happened.'

'Does Kitty work alongside you all the time? I know she mentioned that she is the cook.'

'Not all of the time, but yes, Kitty does much of the food. She doesn't work full time because there's Danny to look after, and he's only eight.' Rob stopped abruptly. 'Sorry,' he added, 'that was insensitive of me mentioning my boy when yours, you know, isn't here anymore.'

'It's alright,' she said in an even voice, and dropped her eyes from his.

He remembered something Kitty had said about when people had lost someone they often wanted to talk about them. 'Your boy, David wasn't it, what was he like?'

Her face seemed to close down as she looked up sharply at him. 'I don't want to talk about David, if you don't mind.' Her voice was still polite, but there was a firmness to it now. 'I'm sorry,' said Rob. 'I won't mention him again.' Secretly he felt relieved.

'Thank you for understanding,' she said. She took a deep slow breath and seemed to will herself to relax and smile. Her skin was like cream. 'While we were riding up here,' she said in her normal courteous tone, 'I spotted a wood that was absolutely covered with snowdrops. Do you think we might stop there on the way back and have a look?'

Their boots crunched over twigs and the remains of last autumn's leaves as they stepped into the wood. You didn't have to go far to see the snowdrops; they were visible from the road if you knew what to look for. Celia was going mad for them, exclaiming and bending down to touch them. They wandered a few steps deeper into the wood.

'They are so beautiful,' she said, her face alight. 'Like a white mist through the trees. And so many of them!'

'You like flowers, then?' he stood stiffly by her, not sure what else to say.

'I absolutely adore flowers,' she said. 'Look, there's a log. Can we sit here a moment, among the snowdrops?'

They sat down, their leather clothing creaking quietly as their movements settled. Rob cast a glance towards where the bike was parked. Yes, he could still see it.

He was aware of her stillness. She had taken her gloves off to touch the snowdrops and her hand lay on the log between them. He took his own gloves off and laid his hand on hers. She didn't move. When they were just sitting quietly like this, there was no sound in the wood. He slid his arm around her and kissed her tentatively. She broke away from the kiss first and laid her head on his shoulder. He hardly dared to breathe.

Before he could kiss her again she said, 'We should be getting back.' They climbed back on the bike in silence and travelled back down the valley to her house.

Rob brought the bike to a halt on her drive. As she took her helmet off she nodded to the car on the drive next door. 'The neighbours are home. That's unusual during the day.' She stood apart from him. 'Thank you again,' she said. 'That was lovely.'

He blurted out, 'Are you going to tell Malcolm about our trip out today?'

He couldn't read her expression. 'Do you want me to?'

Rob had already turned the engine off but she made no move to invite him in. He took a deep breath. 'I'm not going to tell Kitty. I didn't tell her last week either.'

She nodded slowly. 'Alright. It will be our secret.' She looked withdrawn and remote from him now.

'Do you think I could have your phone number? Would you mind if I phoned you and perhaps we could go out again next week?'

He half expected her to say no, but she agreed and told him it was listed in the phone book. His hand hovered over the ignition keys while she watched him with her pale eyes.

'OK, then. I'll phone you.' He revved up the bike and backed it out of the drive. He looked back to wave to her, but she had already gone into her house.

*

'Do you realise that we're more than half way through our training? After today there's only five weeks of full training and then the two weeks taper.' Kitty prided herself on having her finger on the pulse of their training schedule. She did it efficiently, she obviously enjoyed doing it and it meant he didn't have to. So Malcolm simply went along with it.

'My goodness, that must call for a celebration of some sort,' he said as they chugged doggedly along the track. Their feet almost knew the way by now.

'An extra chocolate digestive in the car afterwards?'

'Alas, today I have to leave straightaway after the run today. Our daughter has come to stay for the weekend.'

'Oh… that's a shame.' Kitty had become used to a biscuit and a cup of coffee from Malcolm's flask after their run, a time to start recovering and refuelling, and to reflect, so far with satisfaction, on how the run had gone. It was an intimate interlude. Kitty valued this time before Malcolm dropped her back at *The Spinning Coins* and it was all a mad rush.

'Well,' said Kitty, making sure that her voice was bright, 'That's nice for you both. Adela, isn't it? Has she come for anything special?'

'No, sometimes she just turns up, out of the blue. She can get here quite easily on the train with her Railcard, you see. I think she comes when university life – or more likely her social life - all gets a bit

69

overwhelming for her.' Or if she wants some more money, he could have added.

Adela had arrived yesterday. He had felt the same mix of pride, discomfort and bewilderment that he usually experienced when he was around his daughter nowadays. She was an arresting young woman. Good looking – insofar as he was able to judge objectively – slightly abrasive and certainly impassioned. He really didn't know where she got these character traits from.

She had chattered away excitedly enough and certainly Celia had come out of herself and they had spent time engaged in girly chat and suppressed giggles that left him mutely on the sidelines. She seemed to have forgotten her comment on the phone last time they had spoken, but anyway, he thought it safest not to mention David at all.

He had, however, managed to tell her about his running progress. He remarked as much to Kitty. 'She couldn't believe that her old Dad was going to run eighteen miles this morning,' he said. 'She even looked at me with respect and admiration. Hopefully even more so this coming lunchtime when I can actually boast that I've done it. I shall bask smugly at the dining table.'

'And so you should,' said Kitty, pleased to hear him light-hearted.

'But there isn't any rest for you when you get home, is there? I find that I'm absolutely shattered for the rest of the afternoon.'

'It's a matter of necessity,' she replied. I do get a good rest after the lunchtime session though, and the kitchen isn't open Sunday nights so I get a quiet evening too.' She didn't add that maybe he was more tired because he was older than her. 'Anyway, how did your midweek runs go this week?'

She always asked, and he always had the slight feeling that he was sending in his report. He didn't mind, because without her input he knew that he might well be lazy and not put the miles in.

'They went well,' he said. Three lunchtime runs of four miles, then ten miles – ten! – on Wednesday. I've switched the Wedneday run to first thing in a morning because it's too long to fit into lunchtime now. It felt odd, starting running in the dark. I've bought a reflective tabard, to keep safe on the roads.'

'Well done,' she said. 'I did a midweek ten miler too and the other

70

runs were fives.'

It amused him that she conferred her approval on him. 'Do I get a gold star?' he asked, laughing.

'Wait until you've done twenty-six point two miles,' she said. '*Then* you get your gold star.'

*

Rain. A monotonous grey sky was squeezing out a continuous stream of fat rain drops. Kitty had just set off for the bus stop to meet Tina, grumbling about the weather. The hood of her parka was pulled right up so that she peered out through a tube. Well, I can certainly forget the bike today, thought Rob, looking mournfully through the window.

He had told Kitty that he would probably pick up a few things from the Cash & Carry, so she knew he would be going out. The question was should he phone Celia first, or just go to her house and hope that she was in. He paced up and down in the living room of their flat with his dilemma, like a caged animal. Of course, he could do something else altogether. After all, Sam was coming in to do the lunchtime session as regular thing for the next few weeks. Kitty had queried this, but he said that Sam needed the extra money and was willing to do the overtime. Which was true.

He threw himself down on the sofa and picked up the newspaper. Ten seconds later he dropped it, snatched up the phone, and dialled. She answered on the second ring.

'Hello,' he said, adding his name when she evidently didn't recognise him, and saying all in a rush what a miserable day it was and what a pity there was no chance of a trip out on the bike.

'Ah, yes. It really is a very wintry day. It's more like sleet here than rain.' Her voice, detached as it was on the phone, seemed posher than when he was with her.

His words tumbled over one another as he said that he had to go to the Cash & Carry, and would she like to go out for a cup of coffee or something afterwards? She replied smoothly that why didn't he come to her house for a coffee instead, since he would be passing.

When he put the receiver down he found that his hands were shaking. Ma was in the passageway when he bounded downstairs, and

71

he gave her a smacking kiss on the cheek as he headed out to the car.

*

He sat on the sofa listening to the sounds of the kettle boiling in the kitchen and her heels tapping on the kitchen floor. When she had opened the door to him she had been wearing a knee length skirt and a jumper which, he couldn't help noticing, was just fitting enough to reveal her breasts without clinging to them. She asked him to come in and led the way to the living room. Her heels weren't very high, they were those mini-stiletto ones, thin heels anyway. They made her bottom sway and her calf muscles tense when she walked, and her skirt made a swishy sound against her legs. He thought of the previous time he had been here, sitting on this same sofa and drinking coffee with her. What a surprise it had been to find that he had something in common with this classy woman. He had been so nervous then. As he was now.

That previous time she had sat in the armchair opposite him. Is that where she would choose to sit now when she came in with the coffee? He shuffled restlessly in his seat as he heard her push open the door. She put the tray on the coffee table and sat down on the sofa. Not beside him, but at the other end.

'This is the tapestry I'm working on,' she said as she poured from the pot, indicating with a nod of her head a piece of fabric which lay on the coffee table. 'I was working on it when you arrived.' Rob hadn't noticed it. She picked it up and smoothed it out to show him, laying it on the sofa between them. It was a picture with flowers on it, and she had filled in half of the flowers with tiny little stitches. The fabric felt coarse between his fingers. 'It's good,' he said, aware of the inadequacy of his response.

She picked it up and put it away in the basket alongside the sofa 'I do a lot of embroidery,' she said. 'It helps to pass the time. Would you like a biscuit?'

She picked up the plate.

'No thanks,' he said. She put the plate down and folded her hands in her lap. Neither of them drank their coffee.

Rob moved along the sofa and took her in his arms. Her ripe fruit mouth yielded under his, and he put his hand on her knee, underneath her skirt. When he slid his hand slowly upwards, he found that she was

72

wearing stockings.

*

The church clock struck twice, the sound carrying easily enough through the still night air. Rob sighed and turned over again. The bedroom was in darkness but he could just make out the mound of Kitty's outline next to him. He quietly slid out of bed and fumbled for his slippers and dressing gown, casting a wary eye her way. He didn't want her waking up and asking why he couldn't sleep.

He slumped on the sofa in the living room. For once he wished he still smoked, but he didn't want to start that mug's game again. A whiskey? That would mean going down to the Bar. A mug of cocoa? Then he'd want to pee later.

He leaned his head back against the sofa and closed his eyes. It felt easier to think about Celia when he wasn't lying alongside Kitty. That first time, upstairs in her guest bedroom, she had removed her clothes with her back to him, and he had asked her hoarsely to leave the stockings and suspender belt on. She had turned around and he took in her swaying breasts, nipples like spilt wine, before she slid quickly under the sheet. He had wanted to pull it back so that he could relish the sight of her, but she had protested, so he had to content himself with exploring her skin with his hand, allowing his fingers to sink into the flesh of her belly, tracing her voluptuous curves, trickling his fingers along the lacy edge of her suspender belt and around the silky tops of her stockings. It was almost unbearable.

And twice more after that, on the next two Tuesdays. She was becoming a bit less shy and would let him gaze greedily upon her for a minute or so before she covered herself, but she still thought her body was unattractive. He didn't have the words to tell her that nothing could be further from the truth, that he worshipped the abundance and paleness of her flesh. She was like one of those old paintings that you see.

He had even gone to see her yesterday morning. Knowing that Malcolm was out running with Kitty, he suddenly had to drive frantically to her house, if only for a quarter of an hour. There hadn't been time to do any more than kiss her and burrow his hand under her blouse. He was fumbling with the buttons when she had gently put him

73

from her and said that they had better not go any further, because there wasn't time. He had humbly complied, dropping his hands to his sides while she turned away and discreetly rearranged her clothing. He was just grateful for the privilege of being with her.

He had driven back at top speed, thankfully avoiding a conversation with Ma, because she would have guessed from his face that he was concealing something. Always she'd been able to see through him. But she was nowhere around and so he was safe. There was still about half an hour before Kitty would come back, all flushed and triumphant like she was after these long runs of hers.

And then when he had come to bed a couple of hours ago Kitty was still awake, waiting for him. He had made love to her, hungry from his earlier frustration, and unable not to contrast her lean and toned small body with the way that he seemed to sink into Celia like a welcoming feather bed. And he used to wonder how men who had affairs could come home and be able have sex with their wives.

But it was all worth it, wasn't it? Even if thoughts of her kept him awake. And only one more day until Tuesday, when he would see her again. He noticed how quiet the night was. But then, who would want to be travelling down their road at half past two on a Sunday in winter? Then he thought he heard a car door shut, close by. Round the back of the pub? Surely not. He strained his ears and he thought he heard a voice, or voices. He got up and pulled the curtain back a few inches. There were two cars in the overspill car-park behind the pub, and he saw Sam and a woman, whom he didn't recognise, get out of one of the cars. Sam's car. The woman pulled her coat around herself; it must be cold out there. They kissed briefly and she got into her own car. He heard Sam laugh as he stepped back towards his car again. He saw the flare of a match as Sam lit a cigarette and waved to her as she drove away. Rob dropped the curtain and turned away.

He could feel the surge of his pulse as he clenched his fists. He pulled the curtain back and looked again. Sam was still stood there smoking his cigarette, cool as you like. Rob flung himself downstairs and unlocked the back door. He marched over to Sam, dressing gown, slippers and all.

'What the fuck do you think you're doing in my car-park?'

74

Sam dropped his cigarette. 'Guv! God, you made me jump. What are you doing up in the middle of the night?'

'What am *I* doing? It's my pub, in case you hadn't noticed, so I'll do what the hell I like. And I don't want shagging going on here on my premises. Do your carrying on somewhere else.'

Sam held his hands up and backed away towards his car. 'OK, OK, I'm not likely to see her again anyway. It was just a one-night stand. Calm down, will you?'

It was Sam's smile, that bloody impudent smile, that did it. Rob stepped up to Sam and slammed his forearm across his neck, pinning him against the side of the car. Their faces were so close that Rob could smell the cheap aftershave even over the cigarette on his breath.

'If I ever catch you doing that again I'll beat the living shit out of you *and* you'll be out of a job. Understood?'

That wiped the smile off Sam's face alright. He nodded up and down, eyes bulging and gurgling sounds coming out of his mouth.

Rob abruptly let him go and strode back into the pub. He heard Sam's car driving away as he locked the back door.

A double whiskey wouldn't be enough; he made it a triple. He was half way down the glass before he started to feel anything like normal. He had only put one light on, behind the bar, and the Lounge was in semi-darkness, not even a glow from last night's fire in the grate. His eyes grew accustomed to the gloom and he sat on, motionless, nursing his glass in his hand. He couldn't think anymore.

He crept into the bedroom and slid into bed. He froze as Kitty stirred and mumbled in her sleep, but she didn't wake up. Even with the whiskey, he still stared at the ceiling for another half an hour before he finally dropped off.

Chapter 7

'Ready, then?' said Kitty. 'Couple more calf stretches, perhaps?' Both she and Malcolm released their quad stretch and squatted to stretch their calves, one at a time. 'I love the feeling of my muscle yielding and lengthening,' she said as she set the timer on her watch to zero.

'Well here goes,' said Malcolm. Kitty was bouncing on the spot, like a dog who knows he's about to go out for a walk. She was wearing her rainbow striped Lycra leggings and a black light jacket with yellow stripes down the sleeves. 'You're really excited about this, aren't you?' he said. 'I'm just a tad nervous. If I've got butterflies today, goodness knows what I'll be like on race day.'

'The trick is to get your butterflies to fly in formation, so they say.' She spoke briskly; her energy was bubbling out of her and she was eager to start.

They both pressed their buttons to start their watch timers and glided comfortably into their pace. It was a well-known routine now. Malcolm looked at his watch and saw the seconds unfold. Twenty miles at an eight minute mile pace. That's one-hundred and sixty minutes, or two hours forty minutes. How many seconds is that? He couldn't work it out in his head. Fine accountant you are, he told himself.

'I would never have thought, two months ago, that I would be able to run twenty miles today. At least, I haven't run it yet,' he added.

'We did nineteen miles two weeks ago, so it's only a mile longer than that,' she replied. 'And last week it was only seventeen. So you've definitely got it in your legs. You just have to get it in your head.'

'You're right, as ever,' he said. He glanced across at her as they ran. She reminded him of one of those high-stepping ponies that you sometimes saw in circuses and the like, feisty and spirited, but under control. Without her, he doubted that he would be staying the course.

'Look,' he said. 'Look at the buds on the trees. There are primroses and daffodils in the woods too. Spring is on its way.' Malcolm felt a surge of lightness as he glimpsed the flecks of yellow under the trees. This time last year he had been too warped by grief to notice the advent of spring. Indeed, about three weeks after David had died he had looked at his lengthened fingernails and wondered how it had happened that they had grown without him noticing. That time had been hideous. But now, here he was, probably as fit as he had ever been and in the company of an engaging young woman on a beautiful spring day.

'I do enjoy your company, you know,' he said. She answered predictably enough that she enjoyed his too.

After a pause she added, 'You know what? I think it helps that we're side by side, not face to face.'

'What do you mean?'

'Well, we just talk and listen to each other. It's more..., more *intense*, somehow. When you're looking at someone when they're speaking, sometimes their voice is saying one thing and their face and body language are saying another. And then there's usually other things going on in the background to distract you. With us, we just let our legs get on with it and pour it all into the talking and listening, with only nature around us. I think that's what I mean, anyway.'

Malcolm digested this. 'Yes, I think I understand. We would never have conversations like we do if we were politely sitting across a table. And we wouldn't have met under other circumstances, anyway.' He thought for a moment. 'The physical act of running unites us too. The rhythm. It's almost like a hypnosis.'

'Great, isn't it?' He could hear the smile in her voice.

He dwelt in the sound of their feet on the earth for a few minutes. Then he said, 'So, have you come up with your question for the day? We've had if you were an animal what would you be, what colour would you be and why, what are your top three favourite foods. What else have you got in your book on topics for conversation during long marathon training runs?'

'Yes, I've thought of a question for today. Here goes. Tell me something positive from your week.'

Malcolm blew his cheeks out. 'Just off the top of my head?' He played for time. 'Ah, you've had time to think. Why don't you tell me your positive thing first.'

'OK then. Danny got ten out of ten in his spelling test this week. He often gets seven or eight, but this was the first time he got ten, and I'm really proud of him. We had a special tea with chocolate cake. Oh...' she suddenly stopped. 'I'm sorry. Have I been tactless?'

'No, not at all. I like to hear about your family.' He meant it; her life fascinated him.

'Now your turn,' she said.

Hr groaned. 'Oh dear, you've put me on the spot.' He cast around for something he could parade from his mediocre week, to indulge her. Not only to indulge her, since he actually liked the zany games that they played during their long runs. It meant that he got to know her more, in an oblique way, and it took him out of himself, as they say. As he reviewed his week, a dull panic started to rise. Every day at work he had braced himself to step on the treadmill. Every evening he had gone home to a house drenched in bleakness and obscure reproach. Yesterday he had pottered in the garden and cleaned the car. A barren but typical week, devoid of any real joy. Then he had it, the positive thing he could contribute. 'My midweek semi-long run,' he said. 'I did eleven miles on Wednesday, after work because there wasn't time in the morning, in less than an hour and a half. I felt good when I came home. Like I do after our long run, in fact.'

He felt rather than saw her approval. 'My eleven miler was good too,' she said. 'Except that I did it on the Wednesday morning when it rained, which was a bit miserable. So, your experience was more positive than mine, you see.'

The miles evaporated, part in silence, part in chatting. They said several hellos to other people out running, walking dogs or gingerly supervising young children on bikes with stabilisers. After about nineteen miles Malcolm started to feel weary and said as much to Kitty.

She agreed. 'It's not much further,' she said. 'We're both coping well. But...' She paused.

'What?'

'Well, they do say, in running magazines and books and stuff, that twenty miles is only half way. Effort wise, that is. And for some people it's worse than others, in terms of how the Wall affects them and how their particular metabolism copes with it.'

'I remember you said that the Wall phenomenon is about changing over from glycogen to fat burning, but how exactly does that affect a person? Is it that you feel really tired? I would have thought that's only to be expected in the last few miles of a marathon.'

'Apparently it's not only that. It might mess with your head and your brain doesn't function properly because all your energy is diverted to your muscles, so you can get quite negative...' Her voice trailed off. Then she added 'A bit daunting, isn't it? Sometimes I wonder why I'm doing this.'

Privately Malcolm thought she was over-dramatising the effects of this so-called Wall. He said, 'I don't want to think too much about that final six miles either. But last year I saw hundreds, thousands, of people on television finishing the London Marathon, and they were all shapes and sizes. Surely we're at least as good as they are?'

'You're right,' she said somewhat doubtfully, and then with more conviction, 'Yes, of course you're right. It'll be an effort, but I'm sure we can do it. Look how we're sticking to the training plan. You can't do more than that.'

He was relieved to hear the customary confidence return to her voice. If she lost heart, then he was sure that he would too. She was his inspiration.

They turned a corner and there it was, the white glimmer of his car beneath the trees. Just a few more paces and they would have had done it. Twenty miles.

They both leaned against the car and finished off the rest of their water. They rested, savouring the heaviness in their legs, the gradual slowing of their breathing and the perverse pleasure of physical tiredness justly earned.

'I'm tired but not exhausted,' he said. 'How about you?'

'Same,' she said. They smiled at each other. 'And pleased. Now that we've got this under our belt, I'm sure we can do it.'

He lifted his weary arms – yes, his arms seemed to have got tired as well as his legs – and gave her a hug. She felt tiny, and he smelt the tangy odour of her fresh sweat. As he released her he said, 'I'm proud of us.'

*

Rob heard the sound that he was waiting for: the front door of the pub opening and closing downstairs. Four minutes to seven. Sam was always on time, you could say that about him. Rob pulled his shoes on.

'I'm just popping downstairs to see if Sam's alright,' he said.

Kitty looked up from where she was sitting with Danny on the sofa, hearing him do his reading. One page of the book had a picture of a smiling family having a picnic – Mum, Dad, two kids and a dog – and on the facing page was a written description of this happy scene. Danny was in his blue stripy pyjamas, his face puckered in concentration as he sounded out the words from the book. Kitty was also in her pyjamas, her feet in pink furry slippers resting on the coffee table. Their heads were together over the book, Danny's hair looking darker tonight than Kitty's because it was still damp from the bath. It struck Rob, not for the first time, how alike they were.

'You're going down already? It's not likely to be busy, is it?' said Kitty, her finger on the place where Danny had read to.

'Probably not.' Rob tucked his shirt in. 'But I thought I'd just go and check that everything's OK. I'll come back if it stays quiet.'

Kitty nodded vaguely and returned her attention to Danny's struggles.

Rob shoved Danny lightly on the arm on his way past. 'Off to bed soon, are you, mate?'

Danny looked appealingly at Kitty. 'Yes, you are,' she said. 'It's school tomorrow.'

'Do you know your Mum ran twenty miles today?' Rob added from the doorway. 'She's Supermum!'

'Twenty miles?' echoed Danny. 'Wow! Are you all tired out then?'

'It was actually eighteen miles today,' said Kitty. It was twenty miles last week, and we'll do twenty miles again next week. I was a bit tired this afternoon. But I had a rest and I'm OK now.' She nudged Danny. 'After all, I am Supermum!'

As he walked downstairs Rob heard Danny labouring over his words again, and Kitty encouraging him to sound it out. Poor little sod, he thought. Kitty's so ambitious for him, always wanting him to do well

80

at school, to be better than either of us have been. She's probably right, too.

Sam was just unlocking the front door and latching it open when Rob came in. The clock said exactly seven o' clock.

'Alright?' said Rob.

Sam wheeled round in surprise. He was looking dapper, as always, in a crisply ironed blue shirt and a tie. 'Alright, Guv? I didn't expect you down so early.'

Rob ambled around the Lounge, poking up the fire, lining up chairs. 'No, well, I didn't have anything better to do. Everything OK? How's the family?'

Sam nodded as he lit up a cigarette. 'Grand. Both the kids growing like weeds and Tess is looking at these holiday brochures and coming up with all sorts of ideas we can't afford. You know what they're like.'

To give Sam his due, he was his normal affable self. He didn't seem to be holding a grudge about being half strangled last week. Rob hadn't had a chance to talk to him on his own since the incident, because there had always been customers lurking. And if he didn't get on with it, he'd miss his chance now. So he thrust his hands into his pockets and said, 'Look, Sam, I'm sorry about last Sunday night. I just saw red about…well, about what was happening. But I was well out of line, grabbing hold of you like that.'

Sam shrugged. 'Nah, I was the one out of line. It *is* your pub, like you said.' He broke into one of his trademark cheeky grins and rubbed his hand over his jaw. 'I'm glad you didn't smack me one, though. It might have been difficult to explain at home if I'd had a black eye.'

Rob let out a sigh of relief. Sam could have made things very nasty for him if he'd wanted to; attacking an employee in the workplace wasn't exactly allowed. He didn't think Sam had wanted to follow it up in that way, because he would have said something by now, and he'd been perfectly normal when they had worked together since. Even so, it was good to clear the air.

There still wasn't a soul in the pub, which wasn't that unusual for early on a Sunday night. 'Seriously, Sam. How do you do it? Didn't Tess wonder where you were?'

Sam leaned on his elbow against the side of the bar. 'She was sound asleep when I got back. And even if she hadn't been, she wouldn't have wanted to know.'

'Do you love her?' said Rob, awkwardly. It wasn't the sort of thing that blokes usually said.

'Course I do. We've been married for ten years now. But sometimes... put it like this. Even if you ate caviar at home every day, you'd still fancy going out for fish and chips now and again, wouldn't you? You know what I'm saying?'

Rob nodded slowly. 'Or if you have good home cooked meat and two veg every day, you might still fancy a nice rump steak sometimes.'

Sam gave him an odd look. 'Yes, I suppose.'

'When you put it like that... only you see...' Rob paused. Suddenly he desperately needed to share his secret with someone who would understand, who wouldn't judge him. And a part of him, a part of himself he didn't like very much, wanted to boast, to see the leering admiration in Sam eyes, to see him go up in Sam's estimation.

Their attention was caught by the door of the Lounge opening. Straightaway, Sam stopped listening to Rob and stepped forward to serve the middle-aged couple who came in, giving them all the usual chat about had it come on to rain yet, and so on. Half a minute later two local lads came into the Bar and Rob pulled their pints for them while they set up the dart board. Shit, that was a near thing, he thought. Whatever was I thinking?

'I think I'll go back upstairs for a while and watch a bit of TV with Kitty and the boy. I'll be down about eight, unless you buzz me before.'

'Right you are,' said Sam. 'Oh, and Rob, what we were talking about before...'

Rob turned back reluctantly. 'What about it?'

'Just what the fuck is caviar anyway?'

*

Kitty and Tina waved at the departing school bus. Not that Danny and Luke were looking, they were too busy jostling for seats with their friends.

'I'm glad to see the back of him today,' said Tina. 'He's been a little sod this morning. I had to practically dress him myself.' She sighed. 'And it'll be Easter holidays before we know it. Got time for a coffee?'

82

Kitty shook her head. 'I really haven't, sorry. I've got to squeeze my run in now and then I've got a lot of cooking to do when I get back. Meat pies and lasagnes. We're nearly out.'

'Rather you than me,' said Tina as they set off to walk back.

'The running or the cooking?'

Tina grimaced. 'Both. How's the training going, anyway? It's not long now, is it?'

'Three weeks on Sunday. And it's all dead on schedule, thanks.' Tina always asked. She was a good friend, solid as they come. 'But I'm getting nervous as it's getting closer. And the other thing that's bothering me,' Kitty added, 'is that we haven't yet repaid Malcolm and Celia for the meal we had at their place. We can hardly have them in our kitchen upstairs. I'd be too ashamed after seeing their place. I suppose we could take them out for a meal somewhere, even though it would be expensive.'

'What does Rob say about it?'

'He's not keen at all. When I mention it, he just says it's unnecessary, that they won't expect it and to forget about it. But I want to show them that even though we're not posh like them, we still know our manners.'

Tina pulled a Crunchie bar from her coat pocket. 'Breakfast,' she said cheerily. 'I couldn't eat it in front of Luke, after he's had to put up with Shredded Wheat. Want a bit?'

'No, thanks. So what do you think I should do? About this dinner thing?'

'You could always stand them a meal in your pub.' She took another bite of Crunchie and added through a mouth full of chocolate and honeycomb, 'After all, it's the best ever, your food. Don't worry about all that fancy crap that she can make, you make good wholesome nosh. Just be proud of it, girl. I would be.'

Kitty nodded slowly, as the possibility took shape in her mind. 'That's probably our best bet. I could get Ivy to come in at six and do the kitchen, then if they didn't mind eating early, we could eat with them while Sam watches the Bar. Or, even better, they could come at the end of Sunday lunchtime and we could have a late lunch after the pub closes.' On impulse she put her arm round her friend and kissed her on the cheek. 'Thanks, Teen. You always boost my confidence.'

'We girls got to stick together,' said Tina, stowing her chocolate wrapper back in her pocket.

They parted company at the corner of Tina's road and Kitty did her stretches, feeling a bit self-conscious doing them on the side of the road which ran through the village. One car honked her and called out something through the window that she didn't catch. Well, let them see if they could run fifty miles in a week.

Fifty miles. This was the longest mileage week. She'd packed eleven miles into her legs on Wednesday, yesterday it was five, quite fast, and now she was going to do seven. It's like having another part-time job she thought, as she set off down the street at a gentle warm up pace. It's dominating my life just now. But only three weeks to go.

As usual when she ran nowadays, she mentally went over her progress and her preparation for the forthcoming days. The big focus was the second twenty miler, coming up the day after tomorrow. She and Malcolm had agreed that they would simulate race day as much as possible (she'd read that this was a good idea) by having a high carbohydrate dinner the night before and getting well hydrated, then a high carbohydrate breakfast, also with plenty of water, about two hours before they started running. Of course the actual race would start at 9.30 a.m. on the dot, but they would have to begin their long run on Sunday at 8 a.m. so that Kitty could get back for work. They would be wearing the exactly the same kit that they would wear on the big day, and put plenty of Vaseline on all their body parts that had got rubbed when they did the previous twenty miler – toes, heels, nipples, groins. Kitty hadn't liked to ask Malcolm if he had got sore nipples, but she certainly had.

She turned off down a quiet side road and eased into her regular pace, which was a bit faster than eight minute miles when it wasn't a long run. Yet she had to admit that it wasn't as much fun as it used to be. In the days when it was just running and not marathon training, she used to relax and escape into her head when she ran. It was time out, time on her own, time to let her mind loose, time to merge with the natural world around her. But now she was driven. She had targets to reach, and far more time had to be spent churning out the miles.

And not just completing the miles. There was now also the mental preparation that she had read about. Visualisation, they called it. She had been having a go at it for the last couple of weeks. She started a visualisation now. First she focussed on her breathing and tried to clear away any stray thoughts. Then she allowed a picture to form in her head, a clear picture where she is standing at the start line, poised and ready.

I hear the bang of the starting gun and I am setting off at my normal pace. Everyone around me is relaxed and smiling, like I am. The running flows easily out of me. I am in total harmony with my body. My arms hang relaxed and gently pumping at my sides while my legs keep turning, turning, turning. My body knows exactly what to do. At each mile marker I slow down, take the cup of water that is waiting for me and drink it all down, feeling the coldness flood my stomach and rehydrate me. The miles melt away. Before I know it I have reached Tower Bridge. I see the sparkle of light on the River Thames and I look up at the tall grey towers. I am half way round and I am feeling strong, running better than I ever have done. The crowds are cheering for me. My feet carry me on, on, mile after mile.

The streets of London pass by me. I notice the crowd, the buildings, the other runners, the sky. But nothing distracts me from my goal. I am devouring the miles. My body is fit and ready for this. My breathing is easy and regular as my body takes in the oxygen that it needs. I run lightly over the cobblestones, not allowing them to interrupt my pace, and before I know it am on the Embankment. Not far to go now. There are even more people cheering and clapping. Cheering and clapping for me. Now I am turning onto the long stretch of the Mall and I see Buckingham Palace in front of me. My legs are starting to feel heavy now but I can easily cope. Some runners around me are slowing down, but I keep going at my steady pace. And then I see it. Big Ben. It really isn't far now. I feel a new surge of extra energy which carries me forward towards the finishing line. There it is! I see that the seconds on the clock are ticking away, and that the time recorded on the clock is under four hours. Now I'm there, I'm actually there. I am passing the finishing line and I slow down to a stop. Someone puts a medal around my neck and tells me 'well done.' I can feel the ribbon that holds the medal rough against the sweaty skin on the back of my neck. The medal itself is shiny and it feels cool between my hot fingers.

I have done it. I have run the London Marathon. I have run a sub-four hour London Marathon.

Kitty didn't know if she was doing the visualisation right, but she felt more confident and settled after she had done it than before, so she figured it couldn't be doing any harm and it might be doing some good. She turned back onto the main road through the village and saw the sign of *The Spinning Coins* come into view. *I have run the London Marathon,* she said again to herself. And soon it will be true.

*

Celia insisted on drawing the curtains in her guest room before they went to bed. The neighbours might be able to see in, she said. Rob thought that having the curtains closed in the middle of the day was more of a giveaway, but he wasn't about to argue. As they lay there now the light filtered in through the thin gauzy fabric. Pink affairs, they were, and they cast the room in a rosy glow. Or perhaps there would be a rosy glow even without the curtains.

They lay side by side in the aftermath of sex, their breathing gradually returning to normal and his hand gently kneading the top of her thigh. He couldn't get enough of her plump ampleness.

'Have you been out on your motorcycle lately?' she said after a while.

'There hasn't been much chance. I've been too busy coming here. Not that I mind that.'

'Perhaps we could go out again, some time. Today it would have been lovely with this sunshine.' She turned her face towards the curtain where the sun was trying to filter through.

'Alright,' he said, but a bit reluctantly. If they went out on the bike would there still be time for this?

She was still half turned away from him. 'The light's making your face look all pink,' he said. 'It's nice.'

She turned back to him. Her eyes looked like blue stones with nothing behind them.

'Tell me something about yourself,' he said. 'You ask me about my life, but you never say much about yours.'

'I've told you. I'm not very interesting. I haven't done much with my life.'

'Tell me about your childhood then.' He felt on safe ground with that; a time before she had had her son. 'Did you like school?'

'Yes, I liked school well enough. I liked English, and Art, but

History best of all. They were what I ended up studying at A-level. And I quite liked sports. Hockey in particular. Does that surprise you?'

He hesitated. 'Well, we all change from how we were at school. I know I have.' In fact he did find it hard to imagine this classy woman charging around on a hockey field and getting all sweaty.

She settled back on her pillow. 'I read History at university. Then a year after I graduated I met Malcolm.' They both fell silent. Rob didn't want to hear about Malcolm. Or university, for that matter. He was thinking what else to say when she said, 'Before I went to university, I took a gap year. We went travelling in the South of France, some friends and I. We took trains or hitchhiked sometimes. There were some spells of working – in a vineyard, in a restaurant, that sort of thing – then other times we just soaked up the sun and laughed the days and nights away. I believe it was the best time of my life.'

She'd suddenly lit up. It was like when she had first talked about her Dad on his motorcycle. 'I love the sound of your voice,' he said. How on earth did I get to be here with this woman, he thought. She's like something out of a film. He propped himself up on his elbow and gazed at her face.

'I don't know why you should,' she said. 'It's just a voice. And I'm sorry if I got a bit carried away with my memories just then.'

She was closing down again. That air of sadness that was never far away had wrapped round her once more. Impulsively he leaned down and kissed her gently on the mouth. And then again. This time she reached up and drew him closer to her. His erection wasn't slow to wake up.

Suddenly she stiffened in his arms. 'What was that?' she whispered.

Rob listened. 'What? I can't hear anything.'

She remained tense and alert. 'There it is again. It sounds like someone downstairs.'

Then it was unmistakable. A door opened and a voice called 'hello?'

She gasped. 'Quickly! Get dressed!'

Rob didn't need telling twice. Although, even as he was scrabbling for his underpants he was still able to register that this was the first time he'd actually seen all of Celia naked. He just about caught a quick glimpse of her body before she had snapped her bra round her and disappeared under her dress.

The voice came again. A woman's voice. 'Hello? Anybody home?'

'Coming,' called Celia as she pulled on her shoes. Without looking at Rob she smoothed her hair and hurried downstairs.

Rob fumbled with his shoelaces as he strained his ears to hear the voices downstairs. He heard Celia say what a surprise, and was everything alright? The woman replied, but he couldn't hear what she said.

He went to the window and looked out. It was a big drop to the patio in the back garden, so there was no escape-route there. No drainpipe or anything. 'Shit,' he murmured. What the hell was he going to do?

He crept out onto the landing and listened. He heard sounds of water running and the kettle going on as the conversation continued. So he was marooned here, upstairs in Celia's house. If it wasn't so damn serious it would be funny.

Then he heard Celia coming out of the kitchen. 'I'll see if he's finished,' she was saying. She came upstairs and beckoned him into the bathroom. 'It's Adela, my daughter, come home for a couple of days out of the blue,' she whispered urgently. 'I've said that you're a plumber fixing a leak in the toilet. Come downstairs in a minute and say that you've finished, then go.'

Without another word she turned and went back downstairs. Rob lurked. Everything depended on his playing his plumber's part convincingly. Well, here goes, he thought. He went to the top of the stairs and then, as an afterthought, turned back and flushed the toilet. The touch of realism gave him confidence.

Downstairs he stood in the hall and coughed. The daughter was sitting at the kitchen table, talking. Her voice was similar to Celia's, but shriller. Her back was to the door, and he caught a glimpse of her profile as she turned towards Celia. Her hair was blonde, tied up in a ponytail. She could have been a slimmer version of Celia twenty years ago.

'Ah,' said Celia, coming out of the kitchen and ushering him to the front door. 'Did you manage to fix the problem?' Her voice was like ice. Was this the tone of voice that she would normally use to a tradesman? Rob expected her to add 'my good man.'

'Yes, all done,' he said. 'I don't think you'll have any problems now.'

'I'll see you out,' she said. He glanced back at Adela, who still had her back to him. 'Goodbye, love,' he called out cheerily to her, and turned away before she could reply.

As Celia opened the door he said, 'I'll send you my bill for the jobs I've done this morning, shall I?'

Celia drew a breath and glared helplessly at him. He took pity on her and mouthed 'sorry'.

Rob was smiling all over his face as he drove home. He felt alive, exhilarated. They had got away with it! And, all credit to Celia, that was some pretty quick thinking that she had done back there. Treating him as a tradesman like that, she had played her part brilliantly. Perhaps a bit too well.

Chapter 8

Malcolm's car crunched over the gravel as he turned it into the drive and stopped in front of the house. The grass needs its first spring cut, he thought. I'll be able to do that this Sunday because we're only doing ten miles, so there will be more time. *Only* ten miles! How strange it seemed that he could think that now.

The CD was coming to an end, and he turned the engine off and listened to the final couple of minutes of it with his eyes closed. The final chord died away and he reluctantly opened his eyes. He wanted to stay longer alone inside his car, behind the darkness of his closed eyes, absorbing the piece. Instead he gathered up his briefcase and went to the front door.

'Hello,' he called as the door swung closed behind him and he hung his overcoat on the hall-stand next to the door. Straight away he sensed that something was different, although he couldn't have said what. Celia came out from the living room and instead of the neutral detachment that he had grown accustomed to as a homecoming, she was smiling and vivacious.

'I have a surprise for you,' she said, gesturing that he should go into the living room.

'Hello Dad,' said Adela from the sofa when he went in. 'Surprise, huh?' She was wearing jogging bottoms and a loose T-shirt, her hair was caught up in a ponytail and she was sat with her bare feet tucked under her. She uncurled and stood up to give him a hug. He hugged her back and told her how pleased he was to see her. And he was. She had looked so young sitting there like that, more like the winsome adolescent she used to be not so long ago than the rather prickly young woman who aspired to be sophisticated, which is what she seemed to have become in the last couple of years.

After they had settled down he asked her how she had managed to get away from university. It wasn't the end of term yet, was it? She told him that they didn't break up for the Easter holidays for a couple of weeks yet, but things were a bit quiet at present so she thought she'd pay them a visit for a couple of days.

Celia came in with a bottle of chilled white wine and three glasses. 'To families!' said Adela and they toasted each other. Malcolm sat back in his armchair and basked in the unexpected whirlwind of the jolly, almost celebratory, atmosphere in the house. It felt like the first warm day after a dreary winter.

Suddenly Adela jumped up from the sofa and grabbed her large shoulder bag. 'Nearly forgot,' she said, fishing around inside it. 'I've got you a present.' With a flourish she gave him a brown paper parcel. Intrigued, he ripped it open and found a book entitled *Running your First Marathon*. 'It's not new, I'm afraid,' she said. 'I saw it in a second-hand bookshop.'

Malcolm flicked open the pages and took in the clear presentation, the glossy illustrations. He beamed at his daughter. 'You know how sometimes people say, "that's lovely, it's exactly what I wanted?" Well, actually it really is! I've been meaning to buy a book like this for the last few weeks, but not got round to it. Thank you so much, it's very thoughtful.' He got up to kiss her. 'Now I won't have to rely on Kitty for all the information.'

'Who's Kitty?'

'She's my training partner. We do our long runs together and we'll run the actual race together.' He turned over a few of the pages and saw advice on diet, training plans, and preparation for the big day. Exactly what he needed.

'I've got a friend who's going to run in the London Marathon,' said Adela. 'She trains with a club. Last time I checked in with her, she was out every night, pretty much. Seems like a lot of slog to me.'

Malcolm tore himself away from the book and put it on the coffee table. 'Running with lots of other people doesn't appeal to me. Kitty's the same. But also she would struggle to run with a club because of her job commitments. She's the landlady of a nearby pub. She cooks the meals for the evenings – it's all mainly home cooking - and many lunchtimes too. She doesn't do the cooking for the Sunday lunchtimes, but serves behind the bar instead. When we got onto doing really long runs, it was quite a rush for her to get back and get showered and changed in time. The pub is called *The Spinning Coins*, and it has an excellent reputation around here. Kitty and I have some great conversations, about all sorts of things.' Malcolm drew breath to talk about the games they played to pass the time on the long runs, but on second thoughts he finished off rather lamely with 'Oh, and her husband is the pub landlord, of course.'

Adela raised her eyebrows. She turned to her mother. 'Have you met this Kitty?'

Celia took a sip of her wine before she replied. 'Yes. She and her husband came here for a meal a few weeks ago, so that Kitty and your Dad could put together their grand training plan.' She put her glass down carefully on one of the embossed leather coasters on the coffee table.

'I know!' said Adela, suddenly sitting forward and clapping her hands. 'Let's go and eat at this *Spinning Coins* this evening. You've given it such a hot rating, Dad, and I'd like the chance to meet Kitty too.'

'No,' said Celia. Her hand went to the pearls around her neck.

'Well, it's not a bad idea,' said Malcolm. 'It will save you having to cook, darling.'

'Didn't you say we've been invited there for a late lunch on Sunday, after they close? We don't want to go twice in one week, surely.' Her voice was petulant.

Malcolm suppressed his irritation. 'So does that mean I can go ahead and accept their invitation for Sunday? You didn't seem very enthusiastic, so I haven't rung them back yet to reply.'

She got up abruptly and smoothed her skirt down. 'Well, it will be very late to eat lunch, that's all.'

Adela looked backwards and forwards between her parents in some puzzlement. 'Look,' she said, holding her hands up, 'It's no big deal either way if we eat there or not tonight. God, just chill, will you?' She folded her arms and dug herself into the sofa.

Celia turned to her with a placating smile. 'We're not arguing, darling. It's just something we haven't sorted out yet. Anyway, I've already got some bolognaise sauce out of the freezer for us to eat tonight. Why don't you two have a nice chat while I go and start cooking the pasta.'

'Mum's a bit edgy,' said Adela once they heard the rattle of pans from the kitchen. 'And she seemed a bit flustered when I arrived today. Is she OK?'

Malcolm took a breath to calm down. He didn't want the evening spoiled. He wanted to say, edgy is better than the usual withdrawal. She only comes out of it when you're here. But of course he didn't say any of that. He told her that her Mum was fine; possibly just a bit tired because she didn't always sleep very well.

'It could be a perimenopause thing, you know.'

Malcolm was startled, both because that hadn't entered his head, and also because talking about such things with his daughter - who seemed very knowledgeable - wasn't comfortable for him. They'd never had that sort of relationship. He stared at his shoes and mumbled that presumably it was possible. Was it?

Then after a gulp of wine he asked his standard question about how her studies were going, and if everything else was satisfactory. She replied with variations on her own standard sentences, which glossed airily over everything but actually told him nothing. He surveyed her while she was speaking. She really was a striking girl – no, woman – nowadays, with all the puppy fat gone and her face now defined by angles rather than curves. It struck him that this was the first time he had thought of her as a fully-fledged woman, and it filled him with a kind of nostalgic sadness.

'That phone call we had a few weeks ago.' He stopped abruptly. He had come out with that on a sudden whim and now he didn't know how to go on.

She paused, midway through taking the band out of her ponytail and shaking her hair out around her face. 'What phone call?'

'The one where you said I punish you for being the one still alive. I want to say... I want to say I'm sorry if I've made you feel that way.'

'Oh, that.' She twisted a strand of hair between her fingers. 'It's just that when David was alive you were always praising him up, but I always seemed to have to try so hard to get you to notice me. I know he was really clever and everything, but I always did my best. Then when he died, it got even worse. I seemed to disappear right off your radar and you were, well, like a robot with me.'

Malcolm was appalled. 'My dear, I didn't realise.' He stumbled over his words, and tried to tell her how regretful he was. 'I do think, though,' he added, 'that I was like a robot with everyone at that time. Not that it excuses me. I'll make it up to you.'

She shrugged. 'I don't suppose you meant it. But it did always seem that you had more time for David than for me.'

'But I always loved you equally. I promise you that. Perhaps I found it easier to bond with David, though.' He sighed. 'There I go. Excuses again. It will be different from now on, I promise.'

'Oh, don't beat yourself up. I've survived.' She stretched her arms above her head and then looked at him, head on one side. 'You do seem better now than a few months ago. You seem... I don't know... less frozen.'

He nodded his agreement. 'That's partly the passing of time, I suppose, but also the running. I'm more physically fit and it's given me a focus.'

'And a new friend, I gather.'

'Kitty? Yes, we are friends. Good friends. I've been able to talk to her about David and she's been a great help.'

'And what about Mum? She seems different too this visit. But I can't quite put my finger on it. Is she moving on too? I mean, getting over David?'

Malcolm considered. 'It's hard to know. She hardly talks about him.' He paused, wondering how much to say; the thoughts were hardly formed in his head. 'She was the one who wanted to move away somewhere, to make a fresh start, but I sometimes wonder if that has been the best thing. Perhaps we should have stayed close to our friends and all the things that were familiar.'

Just then Celia put her head round the door. 'It's ready. Will you come and help me carry it through, please?'

Malcolm carried dishes and plates from the kitchen to the dining room, his head reeling from the conversation. He was appalled at himself. Adela was chatting away merrily to Celia, seemingly normal. I will make it up to her, he repeated to himself. Suddenly he yearned to talk to Kitty about it, to unburden himself to her as they padded side by side through the woods, and to hear her down-to-earth response.

'Ooh, good old spag bol,' said Adela, grabbing herself a ladleful of sauce with enthusiasm and tipping it over her spaghetti. 'Real comfort food.'

'Nothing special, I'm afraid,' said Celia, 'Because I wasn't expecting you. It is lovely to have you here, though.'

'I wanted it to be a surprise,' said Adela, through a mouthful of her dinner. 'So Dad,' she added lightly, 'When's the big day? Soon, isn't it?'

Malcolm felt a stab of remorse that she didn't seem to be harbouring a grudge against him. In fact she seemed more open than she had for a long time. Perhaps they had cleared the air.

'A week on Sunday. We're into the taper now.' Malcolm then had to explain that the taper was when you reduce your mileage during the last two weeks, so that your body has a chance to recover from all the hard training and to gather its strength for the big push. 'And you need to eat lots of carbohydrates,' he added. 'Which is why your Mum has kindly given me all this pasta.' Celia inclined her head in acknowledgement.

'I would have thought you had to train right up to the race. A bit like revising for an exam. I thought it would all drain away if you didn't keep training right up to the end,' said Adela.

'Well, tapering is the received wisdom, anyway. I've yet to test it out myself of course. I've simply been following Kitty's instructions. But now I have my own book for guidance.' He patted her hand tentatively and turned to Celia.

'You must have a look at the book that Adela bought me. It's very informative.'

Celia nodded. 'Yes, I must.' Then she looked at him with the usual blankness.

Malcolm rushed in to fill the silence that hovered. 'For the weekend of the Marathon we're going to stay in London with your uncle and aunt. It's been a while since I've seen that brother of mine and so it's good to have an excuse to go and visit.' He added, 'Isn't it, Celia?' and looked at her directly so that she had to add her agreement.

95

'Uncle Howard and Auntie Brenda? Oh, I like them. That will be nice for you. Will you stay there while Dad runs, or will you go and watch the race?'

Celia was carefully twirling her spaghetti round her fork. 'I don't know,' she said. 'We haven't talked about it yet.'

'You should go and watch, Mum. On the television it looks like one huge carnival.'

Malcolm waited for her response. 'We'll see,' was all she said.

They all concentrated on capturing the last bits of spaghetti from their bowls. 'I think we've talked enough about this marathon,' said Malcolm as he placed his fork and spoon in his empty dish.

'Yes,' Celia chimed in. 'Tell us some more of your news, darling. Do you have any exciting plans?'

'Since you mention it, I do actually.'

They waited. Was Adela allowing the suspense to build up? 'It's about the Easter break.' Her smile was stretched, stretched over her face, Malcolm thought.

'It's only a couple of weeks to when it starts, isn't it?' said Malcolm, to help her out.

She nodded and twiddled a piece of hair that hung down in front of her face. 'I'm going Inter-Railing,' she said. 'Starting through France, then Germany, and ending up somewhere in Eastern Europe. You see, I've met someone. His name's Liam and he's a postgrad. We're just going to take a couple of backpacks and off we go.' By the end of the speech the excitement was bubbling out of her and her cheeks were pink.

'And when will you be back?' enquired Celia, her voice controlled. 'Are we going to see you at all over Easter?'

'We'll be away the whole four weeks of the holidays,' she said. 'Well, it's hardly worth going for a week or two, is it?' She looked back and forth between her parents, anxious and yet at the same time primed to be defensive if she had to be.

Celia started to speak, to ask, as Malcolm might have predicted, how long Adela had known this Liam. Malcolm interrupted her and said to Adela, 'That sounds really exciting. Once you leave university and get a job, you won't have the chance to do that sort of thing. So you should do it now.'

'Oh thank you Dad!' her words came out in a joyful rush and she flung her arms around him and hugged him. He could feel the slight trembling in her body, and her heart beating. So that was it, he thought. That was why the surprise visit, and probably that was why the present. That was it.

*

Kitty stripped off her sweaty leggings, top and underwear and stuffed them into the washing basket which was squashed into the corner of the small bathroom, next to the wash-hand basin. She turned the shower on over the bath, and took her watch off to leave it on the window ledge, which was higgledy-piggledy with toothbrushes, a toothpaste tube spilling its contents, roll-on deodorants, packs of aspirins, muscle rubs and Rennies. In the midst of it all a bottle of Matey bubble bath in the guise of a pirate, eye patch and all, grinned at her. It was Danny's favourite. It said 10.35 a.m. on her watch and she could hardly believe it. During the past few weeks she had got used to her shower time on a Sunday morning becoming gradually eroded. After the twenty mile runs it was as much as she could do to have five minutes with Danny, a quick lather up and rinse off, then to gobble down her toast and drink while she dressed neatly for work, hoping that she didn't start sweating again over her clean clothes because she hadn't had time to cool down.

She stepped into the shower, drew the plastic curtain with the sea creatures on it carefully across so that she didn't flood the floor, and allowed the water to soak her scalp and course over her body. She felt oddly discontented and restless. After this morning's run of only ten miles her body was straining for more, craving to be taken to the now accustomed edge where fatigue and euphoria mingled and a tide of endorphins, the happy hormones, saturated her. At least I can have a nice long shower today, she thought. And this time next week, we'll have been running in the Marathon for an hour or so. That means we'll probably be passing the Cutty Sark. She closed her eyes and mentally saw herself striding along with the dense pack of other runners past the famous old ship, all smiling and waving, a party on legs. She couldn't wait. At least, that's what she felt now. At other times she was felled by

97

nerves and had to use all her powers of visualisation to calm herself down and restore her confidence.

During their run this morning, she and Malcolm had been through all this and had shared with each other how they were both feeling this see-saw of nerves and anticipation. They had gone through a checklist of preparations for the big day. Initially they had intended to do this after today's lunch in the pub, but then they realised that they didn't really need to write anything down. It was all firmly in their heads. The rest of the time while they were running Malcolm had been talking about a surprise visit he had had from his daughter. Apparently Celia was put out because the girl wasn't coming home for the Easter holidays. Although Kitty had been sympathetic to Malcolm, she privately thought that at the girl's age – what was she, twenty or so? – why on earth would she want to spend all that time with her parents anyway? And it was four weeks holiday that they got off from university. A whole four weeks! In her opinion, the girl was rather a spoilt little madam, but of course she didn't let Malcolm know her thoughts about that. Kitty helped herself to another squirt of rose-scented shower gel – why not, there was time – and slathered it over her body. On the other hand, the girl had bought Malcolm a book on running, which he was pleased about, and it seemed that she and Malcolm had healed some longstanding tension that they had had between them. Kitty had listened to it all. Reluctantly she turned off the shower and picked up the towel. She noticed that there were grubby marks on it, and wondered when Danny would learn, despite her telling him over and over again, to rinse his hands well before he dried them. Of course, it could also have been Rob.

She threw the towel into the washing basket along with her running kit and went to the bedroom to get done up in tights and a skirt and blouse; the usual Sunday lunchtime gear. She had arranged for Malcolm and Celia to come at about 2.15 p.m. Hopefully most of the customers would be out by half past and they could all sit down together in the Lounge. Ivy would bring them their dinner after they'd had a drink. Kitty had even bought some smoked salmon to make a starter. Four plates with the fish, a slice of lemon and an artistic bit of side salad were sitting self-consciously in the fridge right now. She knew she shouldn't be nervous; after all, the pub churned out Sunday lunches every week and they were always highly praised. Yet this was different. She lifted her chin as she looked at herself in her dressing table mirror. I'm going to show Celia that I can cook too, she thought.

*

They were late. Rob had been glancing at the clock on the mantlepiece of the Lounge since just after two and now it was twenty past. Perhaps they won't come. The thought made him half relieved, yet disappointed that he wouldn't see her and play the game of pretending to be two people who had only met once; a kind of subtle verbal foreplay which would tide him over until he saw her on Tuesday when Kitty went out.

Rob took himself back into the Bar, to chat with Sam and the lingerers there, those sad blokes who didn't have a roast dinner cooked by their missus waiting for them when they got home. They were four of the local boys who were always among the last to leave. Good, regular customers with a large capacity for beer; the bread and butter of the pub trade, his Dad used to say. Although, nowadays it wasn't so much on the wet side but on the food side that the money was really to be made, and they had an increasing turnover there, thanks largely to Kitty's efforts.

Sam looked over his shoulder into the Lounge. 'Looks like the people you're expecting are here,' he said.

'At last,' said Rob. 'Don't mind finishing up for me do you?'

'Nah,' said Sam, amiable as ever. 'This lot won't be long, anyway. Good luck.'

He'd obviously picked up that Rob was not entirely looking forward to the formalities of this lunch. Maybe it was the best shirt that gave it away.

Kitty was taking their coats and showing them to the table, already laid up with paper napkins, cutlery, bread and their own best wine glasses that they kept upstairs. A wedding present, Rob vaguely remembered, that came out once in a blue moon. Rob added his hellos, shaking hands with Malcolm and brushing his lips over Celia's cheek. The waft of her ambushed him; a combination of her soap, make-up, clothes, hair, perfume and, underneath it all, her skin. He let his eyes

99

meet with hers as long as he dared, then he turned to Malcolm and enquired jovially if he was looking forward to the Marathon next Sunday.

Malcolm considered the question seriously. 'On the whole I'm looking forward to it. After all, it is the culmination of all these weeks of hard work. But I'm feeling plenty of trepidation too, I have to say.'

'But we mustn't dwell on the nerves,' broke in Kitty. 'It's all going to be wonderful.' Her speech was fast, brittle, betraying her nervousness. 'Now Celia, would you like to sit here? And Malcolm, you go here.' She directed them to their seats, her movements matching her voice. 'Red or white wine? Sorry, we don't have more choice than that. It's just bog standard house red or white, I'm afraid.' She and Rob had agonised over whether to buy in some special wine for them or to give them the pub wine. In the end they had settled for the plonk.

When they all had wine in their glasses Rob proposed a toast. 'To the London Marathon and all who run in her,' he boomed. 'May it be a huge success.' Their glasses clinked and Rob felt himself relax as the wine joined in his bloodstream the pint he'd had earlier. Kitty went off to get the starters, and returned with Ivy trailing at her heels, both of them bearing the smoked salmon platters. Rob could never really understand what people saw in that pink, slimy fish. Give him a big piece of battered cod any day.

She ate so delicately. His eyes followed the food to her mouth, and then back down to the table as she rested her knife and fork on the side of the plate between each mouthful. Her hands, with their pink-tipped nails, lay on the cutlery like alighted birds. Kitty never wore nail polish like that, although his mother did. She always had, as long as he could remember. He finished his starter in a few mouthfuls and sat back with a piece of thickly buttered French bread.

'This is very good smoked salmon,' said Celia to Kitty. 'Is it popular on your menu?'

'Oh, this isn't on our pub menu,' said Kitty. 'I stick to plainer things, you know, soup, paté, things like that. And it would work out too expensive. Our customers wouldn't want to pay much more than a pound for a starter.'

'And what about your main courses? Do you rely on standard

favourites or do you experiment?'

'Well, funny you should say that. Normally in the week I just do the regulars, fish pie, lasagne, faggots and peas, hotpot, chicken curry and steak – all under three pounds each. There isn't room in the kitchen to do more, considering there's ploughman's and sandwiches as well. But I'm thinking of adding my own recipe for spicy bean casserole to ring the changes a bit, and to add a vegetarian option.'

Celia nodded. 'For your Spring menu?'

'Well, sort of. We don't really do seasonal menus.'

Ivy came in to clear their plates and to bring in their roast chicken with vegetables in side dishes, and by this time the girls were talking like old friends about the ins and outs of various meal options. Kitty, in her comfort zone talking about cookery, settled down and didn't seem so jittery. Rob and Malcolm exchanged tolerant glances - women, eh? - while the topic of how to make a really good batter was being discussed. God, thought Rob, as he helped himself to peas and broccoli, if he only knew. And look at Celia. She was playing her part perfectly again. She was chatting away with poise and confidence. What an actress. What a woman. He took a long, satisfying draft of his wine and felt a huge kick as he looked at his wife and mistress talking together. His blood pounded rich in his veins and his chest swelled.

'That really was very good,' said Malcolm as he placed his knife and fork down on his empty plate. 'When I mentioned *The Spinning Coins* at work, one or two people knew of it and said what a well-kept pub it is, with excellent beer.'

'Not that I'm any expert, but it does seem to have a cosy and welcoming atmosphere,' added Celia.

Rob acknowledged the compliments greedily; he was always ready to hear good things about his pub. His eyes met Kitty's across the table with a slight raising of his eyebrows. She acknowledged with a tiny nod of her head.

Rob cleared his throat and fiddled with his cutlery. 'Actually, we're hoping that we might try getting into The Good Pub Guide soon. In the Lucky Dip section to start with, of course. Almost nobody goes straight into the main section. That's why I'm holding out on keeping the beer at under a pound a pint, and why Kitty is adding a new menu item. We could even consider making the Lounge no smoking – that's the latest trend - but I don't know how that would go down with the regulars.'

'How do you get in this Guide?' asked Malcolm.

'By written recommendation, followed up by a secret inspection from someone employed by the Guide, if they think it's worth it,' Rob told him.

'Well, I'll certainly recommend you,' said Malcolm straightaway. 'I can put my hand on my heart and write a glowing report. I could probably persuade one of my colleagues to do so too.'

Rob's mouth fell open. 'Do you mean it?'

'But of course! I'll do it this week. After all, just at the moment I have somewhat more free time than I've been used to these last few weeks.' He smiled at Kitty as he said this.

Rob stammered his thanks. He didn't know what to say. Kitty had said she thought that Malcolm would recommend them for the Guide, but he hadn't really believed her.

By the time they had got to the end of their meals, with empty dessert dishes in front of them, the topic had inevitably turned to the Marathon next week. 'I hear you're staying with relatives in London the night before the Marathon,' said Kitty. Celia confirmed that they were, although they couldn't stay the Sunday night because they had heard this morning that her brother-in-law and his wife were going away on the Sunday for the week coming up to Easter. 'So I'll be left to my own devices during the day. Malcolm thinks it's unlikely that I'll spot him running, with there being thousands of entrants. So I'm not sure what I'll do. Where are you staying?' she asked Kitty.

'I've got a hotel booked near the centre, and then there's a coach laid on to get to Greenwich for the start. It's costing a bomb though, and I've got to pay for the whole double room even though it will only be me in it. Rob doesn't think he would be able to leave the pub.'

'Hang on, I don't know for sure about that,' said Rob. 'I wonder if Sam could lock up on the Saturday, and we could get some extra staff on. I'm sure Ma would love to have Danny all to herself for a night.'

Kitty turned to him in blank surprise. 'I thought you didn't want to come.'

'I never said I didn't *want* to. I didn't think I could swing it, that's all. And it does seem a shame to be paying all that money for the room and not getting the proper use out of it.'

'The Marathon is supposed to be quite a spectacle to watch,' said Malcolm. 'Perhaps you and Celia could team up to keep each other company.'

Before Rob could answer they were interrupted by the outside door slamming and Danny bounded in, anorak hanging off his shoulders and cheeks ruddy and glowing from exercise. He ran up to Kitty and scanned the table, looking for any signs of remaining dessert.

'Hello sweetie,' she said, putting her arm round him and kissing the top of his head. 'Say hello nicely to Malcolm and Celia. Mummy's going to run the Marathon with Malcolm next week.'

Danny burrowed his face into Kitty's side while Malcolm and Celia made encouraging noises to him.

'Come on,' said Rob, irritation showing in his voice, 'You're not that shy. Say hello like a big boy. And where's Granny?'

'I'm here,' they heard. Doris was slightly breathless as she came in, her coat over her arm. Her smile was guarded as she surveyed the table and the company round it. 'We've been for a walk.'

Rob immediately jumped up and stood by his mother. 'Ma, this is Malcolm and Celia. Malcolm's going to run the Marathon with Kitty next week. I told you they were coming to lunch, remember?' He linked his arm with hers. 'This is Doris, my mother. She and my father kept the pub before me.'

Malcolm had stood up when she approached the table. She responded to this old-fashioned gesture with an approving nod of her head then she indicated the empty pudding dishes. 'It looks like you enjoyed your meals,' she said. Unaware that he had been holding it, Rob let out his breath.

Celia was the first to reply, her voice pleasant. 'We certainly did. It was an excellent Sunday lunch.'

'Rob was just telling us that he's hoping to get into the next edition of The Good Pub Guide. We would certainly be happy to endorse that,' added Malcolm.

'There wasn't any of this Good Pub Guide business in my day,' said

Doris. 'Everybody knew it was good pub anyway. We never did meals back then, just a few rolls and crisps. But I'll tell you what, my husband always kept an excellent pint. *That's* the secret of a good pub.'

'And now you have good food too,' said Malcolm.

'Well, yes,' said Doris. 'Rob's done so well since he took over.'

Rob glanced at Kitty and caught the grim expression in her eyes, behind the tight smile. 'Kitty's responsible for all the food side,' he added quickly. 'It's all down to her hard work and planning.' *I'm always having to juggle to keep the two women in my life happy,* he thought with some exasperation. *Keep them apart as much as possible is what works best. And now there's a third woman.* Celia was sitting up straight and elegant, like she always did, looking serenely at Ma but politely keeping her thoughts unreadable.

'When you came in we were just talking about the Marathon next weekend,' Rob went on. 'Ma, if I can get staff to cover the pub so that I could go along as well to keep Kitty company on the Saturday night, do you think you could look after Danny?'

'I'll be virtually looking after him anyway, even if you're here,' she replied. 'So it doesn't make much difference. And maybe things will get back to normal after this Marathon. I'd rather you than me.' The last remark was presumably aimed at Kitty and Malcolm.

Kitty pushed her chair back abruptly. 'If you'll all excuse me, I'm going to take Danny upstairs now.' Rob groaned to himself. He could already predict the conversation that would follow later. *Does your mother have to be so rude? Doesn't she give me credit for anything?*

She said her goodbyes and led Danny briskly away by the hand. Ma, all smiles, said how nice it had been to meet them both and now she was going to put her feet up and have a bit of peace. Danny was a lovely boy but he could be exhausting.

Malcolm stood up and said he needed to visit the men's room. Rob waited for his footsteps down the corridor to fade then he turned urgently to Celia, across the table.

'If I do manage to come to London on Sunday, could we spend the day together?' he whispered urgently.

She nodded.

'Perhaps I could book a hotel room. Yes. Yes, I could do that.' His voice started to rise with his excitement at the plan. She gently put her finger on his lips to quiet him. He caught her hand and pressed it, leaning across the table to stroke her cheek with his other hand.

The noise behind him was faint, but enough to make him jump apart from Celia and turn around. There was no mistaking what he heard next: the sound of footsteps retreating in the direction of his mother's cottage.

Chapter 9

Rob stood by the window looking down at the car-park and the road beyond, blinds half slanted so that Kitty wouldn't see him if she looked up. The rain was bouncing savagely off the road and a couple of cars, probably on their morning commute to work, slurped by with their windscreen wipers lashing. It had seemed like ages, but it couldn't have been more than half a minute, between the muffled sound of the back door slamming downstairs and Kitty's appearance outside, head down against the rain, drawing her hood up as she went. He watched her run up the road until she was out of sight. Then he snatched up the phone.

Her voice always sounded so cool on the phone. Detached and wary.

'Celia, it's me.' When she didn't reply straight away he added, 'It's Rob.'

'Hello. Is anything the matter?'

'Yes. I'm sorry but I can't come round this morning. Kitty's not going out with her friend because she's got a cold. The friend, that is, not Kitty,' he added, feeling silly as soon as he'd said it. 'There was no way I could persuade her to go out somewhere else. I tried, honestly. I'm gutted. Sorry…' he finished off, realising he was starting to grovel.

'Oh dear. Well, that's rather a pity.'

'I know.' He wished she sounded a bit more disappointed. As disappointed as he was.

'Did you book a hotel for Sunday in London?'

'No. No, not yet. But I will. I'll do it today. And I'll let you know where we can meet.' The truth was, there was hardly any accommodation left in central London because of the Marathon, and what was left was eye-wateringly expensive. Plus he had realised that he would have to get somewhere with a late check-out so that they could stay until about 1 o'clock. He needed a miracle on the hotel front.

'Very well.' She sounded sulky.

He made an attempt to be cheerful. 'So, I guess we just have to wait until Sunday. At least we'll have a long time together then while they're doing their Marathon.' He didn't hear her reply because there was a sharp knock on the door of the flat. Without waiting for a response, his mother walked in.

*

Kitty passed the familiar landmarks, *Clarke's Family Butchers* on her right and the baker's and hairdresser's on her left. Then at the end of the main street came *The Bear*, and Kitty noticed with the usual satisfaction how inferior it looked compared to *The Spinning Coins*. The paint was peeling and the car-park was tiny. Her feet then took her down the track alongside the field, where the sleepy sheep were still chewing the grass indifferently, as they always were when she ran this way, her four mile route. Only four miles today! Her body had got used to seven miles on a Tuesday and eleven on a Wednesday, so she hadn't run this four mile route for a while. So it would be just a gentle three miles tomorrow and Thursday to keep her legs loose, then resting, hydrating and carbo loading as much as possible on Friday and Saturday. I've done all I can, she thought. I've done the training all to the book.

She had not had the best start to her morning, and she felt decidedly irritable. She tried to settle into the run and let the tempo of her feet soothe her, but it was raining cats and dogs, which was never the best weather to run in. Let's hope it's better than this on Sunday, she thought.

Everything had been fine, a normal morning which mainly involved urging Danny to hurry up and get ready for school, until she met Tina at the school bus stop. Tina had a streaming cold – or perhaps even the start of flu - and was dolefully sneezing and shivering, her eyes bleary and her nose red. She was feeling so poorly that she had to cry off their usual Tuesday spree to town. Kitty was disappointed, but worse than that, she hoped she wouldn't catch Tina's cold. It was going to be hard enough to run this marathon without a cold, but trying to run it while you're feverish – well, that was the last thing she wanted. So she had tried to edge away from Tina's soggy tissue and had kept as big a distance as she could from her when they walked back. She'd still asked Tina if she wanted any help, though; after all Tina was her best friend. But she had to say she was relieved when Tina declined her offer and said she was going home to lie on the sofa with a magazine and feel sorry for herself.

Then there was Rob. When she had come home and told him that she and Tina weren't going out today for their usual, he had acted really strangely. For some reason he had tried to persuade her still to go, to go on her own, in fact. She had told him the whole point was to have a good gossip and a giggle with Tina. She didn't want to go sitting and eating on her own in some pub. She'd asked him why didn't he come out for lunch, since they still had Sam coming in to do Tuesday lunchtimes, but he didn't want to do that either. Perhaps he was just grumpy because he couldn't take his motorbike out in all this rain. They'd ended up having a spat, with him telling her that she was a bad tempered cow because of all this tapering nonsense, and he'd be glad when this marathon was over, and her telling him that he was just bad tempered for no reason at all that she could see. Then she had flung on her running jacket and banged out of the pub, stomping past Doris and Maisie with only a curt greeting.

Anyway. It might be raining and she might have an irritable git for a husband, but still, she was out running in the fresh air in this beautiful countryside, she was fit and well, and she was ready for the challenge in five days' time. No-one could expect more. And now here she was, at the foot of the hill climb. She launched herself at the ascent up the side of the ridge, feeling her heartbeat and breathing increase in response to the extra work that she was asking of her muscles. Her thighs were singing with fatigue and build-up of lactic acid as she crested the ridge. I haven't done enough of this lately, she thought, chest heaving as she pulled the oxygen into her lungs. It's all been about packing miles into my legs, not speed and short-term effort. She paused, gasping, at the top of the ridge, as had used to be her habit. She screwed up her eyes to try to discern the lazy curves of the river in the valley, but the rain and mist were obscuring it. When was the last time I ran up here this hard? she thought. Then she remembered; it had been the day when there was that to-do with Doris about the Christmas decorations. And now it's nearly Easter already. More importantly, it had been the day when she had got home and the acceptance letter for the London Marathon was waiting for her. She had hardly dared to hope that she would get in.

Then she had also run up here with Malcolm, the second time that they had run together. She hadn't been running flat out that time, because she didn't know what his capabilities were. Also it had been part of a long run, when you didn't push yourself to the limit up hills. Poor Malcolm. She remembered his breakdown, his raw anguish, that day. It made any problems and irritations of her own look small. Yet over the weeks his spirits had improved so much, and their long runs had become an oasis for them both; an escape from the grind of daily life. She liked to think that it wasn't only the running that had helped him.

She started her descent from the ridge feeling less ruffled and more positive. The rhythm, the natural environment, and those magic little endorphins that surged through her bloodstream had all served to uplift and calm her. Let's see what mood His Lordship is in when I get back, she thought. I might as well be the peacemaker, though. That and keep out of his way until his funny mood has passed. After all, it never takes long. I know what I'll do now that I'm not going out with Tina. I'll turn out that cupboard in Danny's room like I've been meaning to do for ages. It's full of old baby clothes and what-not that I can't see me ever using again. Yes, that's what I'll do.

Running. It never failed her.

*

Rob dropped the phone as if it had become hot. He bent down and fumbled to retrieve it, giving himself a chance to cover his confusion. 'Ma. I didn't hear you come upstairs.' He licked his lips.

She advanced into the room, pendant earrings swinging below her hair, which was set stiff with hairspray like a grey helmet. 'Were you talking to *her*?' Her voice was like a bacon slicer.

Rob had managed to avoid his mother yesterday, on his day off, and he had almost convinced himself that she hadn't seen anything on Sunday, that maybe from her vantage point all she could see had been him and Celia talking across the table. No such luck, it seemed.

109

'I don't know what you mean.' He could hear his own voice quavering.

'Oh, please.' She folded her arms tight across her bosom. 'You never could fool me. I saw you on Sunday. I saw you touching each other and looking into each other's eyes like a pair of lovesick teenagers.' She fixed her gaze onto him. 'What's going on, Robert? Tell me.'

Rob broke his gaze away from hers and looked down at the floor. He felt the sweat prickle in his armpits. 'Nothing's going on. Nothing serious, anyway. Just a bit of flirting, that's all.'

He dared to lift his eyes up to her, and she was still nailing him with that look, the one that still could make him shrivel with fear, grown man though he was.

'Think I was born yesterday, do you? I can always tell when you're lying so you might as well tell me the truth right now.' She was on the warpath alright. There was no chance he was going to get off easy.

Rob moved his head from side to side like an animal in pain. He was ten years old again and trying to hide the evidence of his misdemeanours from her. But she had always got everything out of him in the end.

'I'm waiting,' she said, arms still crossed.

'Alright,' Rob burst out. 'We've been meeting up for the past few weeks, on Tuesdays when Kitty's out. It started when I took my motorbike to show Celia because her Dad was a keen motorcyclist. We went out on the bike and, well… things just happened.' He flopped down on the sofa and covered his face with his hands.

'You fool.' He shrank from the scorn in her voice. 'What's a smart piece like that doing with the likes of you? And she's a lot older than you. You're just her toy boy and a bit of rough into the bargain.' Doris shook her head. 'Oh, I can see it all. And you fell for it.'

'No. It's not like that. She's a magnificent woman.'

His mother stood over him, surveyed him with contempt. He hunched in his seat. 'Are you going to tell Kitty?' He felt his world unzipping. If Kitty knew, all hell would break loose. Who knows what would happen.

'Oh, come on, what do you take me for? Kitty might leave and take

Danny with her and then where would you be? No, *I'm* not going to tell her, but you can bet your life she'll find out before long. You'll make another slip sooner or later or she'll find out from somebody else. You can't keep anything secret around here.'

All Rob took in was that she wasn't going to tell Kitty. He felt dizzy with relief.

She sat down in the chair opposite him. 'Oh, I've seen this all before,' she said, sounding more weary now than contemptuous. 'Someone would be playing around and it would be all round the pub almost before he could get his trousers back on. Often it petered out before any lasting harm was done, but sometimes...' She was gazing across the room at nothing, her face heavy. 'Then there was that floozy that your father took up with.'

Rob stiffened. 'I don't want to hear it, Ma. Please.' He wanted to put his hands over his ears, like he did all those years ago in his boyhood when half-understood, half-heard shouting and banging between his parents would drift up to him late at night as he lay in his bed, eyes wide in the clinging darkness, unable to escape. He pushed the memory away, but as soon as he did others crowded in of the grim coldness between his parents that would follow, eventually giving way to an indifference that became normal. He had always known and not known.

She swivelled her gaze back to him. 'It has to stop. Now.' Her voice was quiet, but it was a command nonetheless.

It has to stop, Rob repeated to himself dully. Ma says so, and she's always right. I have to do what she says. Anything for a quiet life. An echo of his father. He bowed his head away from the searing power of her eyes.

But I don't want stop. I *can't* stop. It's something I have that's mine, not just doing what other people expect. *Why* do I have to do what she says?

'No,' he said to her, and surprised himself. He clenched his fists and said it again. This time he looked her in the eye. 'I'll do what I choose, not what you tell me.' His breath was tight in his chest but he made himself carry on looking at her.

He stood up. She looked small, now that he was standing over her.

She started to reply but he talked over her, blocking out what she was saying. 'I've always done what you told me to. I've always given in to you. I took over the pub because it was what you wanted. Yes, I've made a good job of it, but it was never what I chose for myself.' His voice was rising and now he was all but shouting. 'Well, I've had enough. Do you hear?'

'Don't you dare raise your voice to me. You sit right back down there.'

They continued to lock eyes for a few seconds more before Rob turned away from her and marched out of his own sitting room, leaving her there alone.

*

Malcolm cast his eye over the collection of things that he had laid on the bed next to his overnight bag. This included the all-important running shoes, his most comfy running shorts and top, underwear that had been tried and tested for minimum chafing, safety pins to affix his running number to his top, the sweat bands that he had taken to wearing around his wrist and forehead as the weather warmed up, a jar of Vaseline, second choice shorts and top, two pairs of socks and official paperwork with all the instructions. There was also a bin liner, which Kitty had advised ripping a neck and arm holes in as a sort of a jacket to wear while waiting for the race to start, and which could be cast off when they started running. Presumably there would be a battalion of people who cleaned up the rubbish after the receding tide of runners. His other things, pyjamas, shaver, toothbrush and the like, received only a cursory glance. They were banal items, not part of the hallowed Marathon paraphernalia. He picked up his running shoes, their shape after all these weeks a facsimile of his feet, and sniffed their insides. The smell was musty, comforting, redolent of the satisfaction he felt when he peeled them off after eighteen or twenty miles of hard slog.

The phone rang downstairs, and Celia picked it up on the second ring. He could just about hear the murmur of her voice, and then her footsteps to the bottom of the stairs.

'Malcolm? Phone call for you.'

Malcolm padded downstairs and picked up the receiver in the hall.

Celia had disappeared back to the kitchen and he heard the clinking of dinner plates and cutlery being loaded into the dishwasher.

'Hello?'

'Malcolm, it's me. Are you all packed and ready to leave in the morning?' Kitty's voice sounded breathy, her words clipped.

'Nearly. I was just putting things in my bag when you phoned. What about you?'

'I can do my packing tomorrow morning. We're not setting off until after the lunchtime session tomorrow because Saturday lunch is often busy. And anyway, it's getting on for seven o'clock now and the kitchen opens then, so there's no time this evening because I'm cooking.' Her speech had accelerated and she was almost gabbling by the end.

Malcolm settled himself down on the phone seat, next to the little table with the notepad and several pens in a holder. "Maze Hill Station - Malcolm" was scribbled on the pad, in Celia's writing.

'Poor you, working tonight when you should be resting.' He had picked the pad up and was looking at the words in some puzzlement.

'Ideally yes, but there isn't any choice.'

He assumed that the touchiness in her voice wasn't aimed at him. 'So how has it been these last couple of days?' he said. 'I do hope you've been getting *some* rest.'

He heard her expel her breath in a great sigh. 'Oh, it's been horrid this week. I never thought this taper would be so difficult. I feel jittery, irritable, restless, nervous, tense… is that how you feel?'

He gauged how to reply. In fact he didn't feel too bad, and work had been particularly busy so that had taken his mind off everything else. Yet he wanted to show solidarity with her. 'It's certainly been a different week. But there's only tomorrow to get through now. I'm sure it's normal to have the jitters. Anyway, have you been carbo loading and drinking plenty of water, just like you advised me to?'

'That's the easy bit. Lots of toast for breakfast, a huge plate of pasta for lunch and now lean chicken, veg and a big plate of mashed potatoes for tea with a pint of water. How about you?'

'Ditto, pretty much. You mentioned pasta. Will you be going to the runners' Pasta Party tomorrow night?'

The distraction worked. She sounded calmer and more cheerful when she replied, 'Oh yes. Seeing lots of other runners will put me in the right mood. And it's supposed to be really good fun, with music and everything.'

'I can't go because we'll be at my brother's. You'll have to eat my pasta too.'

'Give me your ticket and I might.' They both laughed, the tension eased. She added, 'Just think, in two days' time it will all be over. One of the most important days of my life will be over.'

Malcolm was startled to hear the Marathon described like that. Then he realised that it was, it actually was one of the most important days of his life. 'Yes,' he said. 'It's that level of importance for me too.' He made a mental note to ask her, while they were passing the time in the long hours of the Marathon, what the other important days of her life had been. But then she'd ask him and he wouldn't know how to reply.

'Do you think we'll manage to finish it in four hours?' she asked.

'Well, we think we've maintained eight minute miles during our twenty mile runs. That's three hours forty minutes. That leaves one hour twenty minutes for the last six miles. Surely we can do that.'

'They do say the last few miles is really tough. But imagine, doing a sub-four Marathon!'

'Kitty my dear, I shall be happy just to finish the race and still be standing.'

They both fell silent, contemplating the enormity of the endeavour they were about to undertake. Malcolm was still fingering the notepad with its cryptic message. Then it clicked into place. It was a message that Celia had taken from his brother. He had said he would suggest a place where Malcolm and Kitty could meet before the Marathon. Malcolm passed this information on to Kitty, and they agreed that they would meet at this station at 8 o'clock.

'I guess that's it then,' said Kitty. 'See you at Maze Street station, 8 a.m. on Sunday.'

'You certainly will.' The ridiculous memory of *see you in church* that people would say before a wedding popped into his mind. He had probably said it before his own wedding, in fact. Kitty's statement seemed to carry the same gravitas.

'And remember,' he said, 'the hay is in the barn.'

'What?'

'The hay is in the barn. I read it in the marathon book that Adela gave me. We've done all the hard worked and our harvest is there waiting for us.'

'Yes,' said Kitty. 'The hay is in the barn.'

Chapter 10

Kitty was glad she'd put her track suit on. She had wondered what she should wear for the Pasta Party – jeans or jogging gear - and it seemed that her instinct was correct. She stood in a queue with what seemed like hundreds of other people, who were mostly in assorted sports kit. It was noisy; the hubbub of excited voices competed with sounds of *Keep on Running,* by The Spencer Davis Group, blaring from the loudspeakers. She gulped from a large plastic cup of water as the queue inched forward towards where the pasta meal was being served. The savoury smell engulfed her and made her feel hungry, which was just as well because she knew she had to carbo load like mad this evening. And hydrate, she reminded herself, taking another mouthful of water.

She got to the front of the queue and gratefully took a plate of steaming pasta shapes encased in a rich tomato sauce. Lovely. She moved away to the side of the room to eat and to look around her. The party had been open for a couple of hours or so and it was in full swing, although many were leaving already. Probably they wanted to get back to their various hotels early and have a good night's sleep. Some of the partygoers were in groups, laughing and chatting, while others, like her, were alone and hovered self-consciously around the edges of the room, trying to belong but not quite knowing how.

The pasta was tasty and she ate it eagerly while she mentally reviewed her day. Well, so far so good in her big adventure. She and Rob had got away from the pub straight after stop-tap at two-thirty, leaving Sam to finish up. The journey to London had been uneventful and they had made good time to their hotel. Kitty's eyes had nearly popped out at the lavishness of the hotel foyer, with its deep armchairs and arrangements of fake flowers. She realised that on the scale of hotels in London this one probably wasn't that posh, but even so, she had rarely stayed in a hotel and so to her it was hugely exciting, what with the ultra-polite staff behind the reception desk, a lift that purred up to their fifth floor, an en-suite bathroom, free little shampoos, fluffy towels and a big bed to sprawl on. Not that she spent more than a couple of minutes doing that; she had to go out almost straightaway to get to the Pasta Party. She had asked Rob rather tentatively if he was OK being left on his own for a bit, and he was. He said he'd grab something from the Bar, and that he couldn't remember the last time he'd been able to watch a bit of live Saturday night telly. It would be a treat. He was happy enough, it seemed.

In fact, she was really pleased that Rob had come with her to London. Partly because it was nice to have his support, even though they had decided that it wasn't worth him trying to look out for her tomorrow in the Marathon, what with there being 35,000 runners. The other reason was that he rarely took extra time off work, and the change would do him good. Sometimes he seemed a bit moody lately.

Kitty was brought back to the present moment by a woman who had brushed against her. 'Oh, I'm sorry, I'm just trying to find some space to eat my pasta. I didn't expect it to be so crowded.'

Kitty agreed. They stood together, eating awkwardly. The woman was probably in her thirties too, Kitty guessed, but a bit shorter than she was and carrying more weight.

'It's good to meet somebody else who's here on their own,' said the woman. 'It's my first marathon and I'm wondering what on earth I'm letting myself in for.'

Kitty told her that she was a marathon virgin too and the woman practically fell on her in her delight at meeting someone in the same position. They exchanged stories, and the woman told Kitty that she had applied for the Marathon as a dare, never expecting to actually get in. Kitty was amused to find herself, with her total lack of experience, in the role of giving reassurance and confidence to this poor woman, who did seem to be in quite a state.

'What time are you hoping for?' asked Kitty.

'I'm not really sure. I was thinking maybe five hours?'

Kitty nodded and looked down at the floor to hide her exultation. I could practically walk it in that time, she thought. 'What time did you take to do twenty miles?' she asked.

'Oh, I've only managed to do fourteen miles. What with the kids and everything, I haven't done as much training as I thought I would.'

Lady, you're going to struggle, was what Kitty thought, but she kept that to herself. They chatted for a few more minutes as they finished their meal. Before she left Kitty wished her good luck and said she would look out for her tomorrow.

Kitty stepped out into the mild London evening, exchanging the good-humoured clamour of the Pasta Party for the traffic rumble and fumes in the city streets. She was smiling, her footsteps were firm on the pavement and her head was held high. I can do this thing, she thought.

*

Malcolm closed the bathroom door as quietly as he could. No-one else seemed to be awake yet, but he had not been able to sleep past five o'clock, so at six he had given up and gone to have a shower. The shower was capricious; it alternated between belching scalding water and then suddenly deciding to switch to an icy trickle. The bathroom itself exuded a slightly musty smell, and there was a grimy film over the wash-hand basin. The cheerful rumbustiousness of his brother's house and lifestyle had always slightly unsettled him. It was altogether bohemian, unbuttoned, and not what he was used to in his own conventional life. He hadn't been to Howard and Brenda's house for more than a year, not since before David died in fact, and he was struck, as always, by how different he and his younger brother were. Howard had had a variety of jobs whereas Malcolm had stuck diligently to his accounting. Howard took risks and it invariably seemed to work out somehow whereas Malcolm stuck to what was safe. Howard lived in the moment whereas Malcolm lived in a world of 'what ifs'. These thoughts had always been vaguely in the background when he saw his brother, but this time they nagged at him more urgently and he found himself admitting a sneaking half-desire to be more like him. Was that because of the Marathon, or for other reasons?

He crept back into the bedroom where Celia was still sleeping. So as not to disturb her he had already put on his running kit in the bathroom, and he caught a glimpse of himself in the wardrobe mirror, his legs protruding palely beneath his shorts and his arms skinny by his sides. Do I look in the slightest like a marathon runner, an athlete, he thought? Or do I simply look like a man on the brink of middle age who's fooling himself? He turned away from his reflection and looked out of the window at the jagged rows of roofs that clustered densely in the London suburb. He took a couple of deep breaths but still the tightness in his chest remained.

He checked the time. In an hour Howard would be driving him to the meeting place with Kitty. So there was plenty of time for him to go downstairs to eat a solitary breakfast, which he hoped would help to calm his nerves. Last night Brenda, dressed in a flowing kaftan, had waved a casual hand as they sat amongst the debris of their dinner picnic and told him to help himself to whatever he could find in the kitchen the next morning. He hoped he would at least find bread and coffee. After he had eaten he would bring a cup of tea up for Celia. There was no need to wake her yet as she wasn't coming with him to the Marathon start. Instead she was going on the train to meet up with Rob in the city centre. He looked at her from across the bedroom. She was lying on her side, one hand cupping her cheek, which was a familiar sleeping position for her. He moved closer, taking care to make no noise, until he could see clearly the lines that had recently begun to etch themselves around her eyes and mouth. I will tell her, he thought. If the Marathon goes well, I will tell her. No, he corrected himself. I will tell her anyway.

*

'How are you feeling?' said Rob, drying himself briskly on the towel as he emerged from the bathroom.

'Do you know what, I feel OK,' said Kitty. 'Not particularly nervous at all.' The hotel room was quite small, but it was big enough for her to do a few stretches and lunges next to the rumpled bed. She exhaled slowly and brought her arms down gracefully from a sideways stretch. Then she jogged up and down on the spot.

Rob took a mouthful of the coffee that she had made for him using the little kettle in the room. 'I feel tired just looking at you,' he said, and pulled on his boxers. 'Aren't you supposed to be conserving your energy or something?'

'I think I'm as conserved as I can get.' She lunged into a calf stretch. 'Now all I want to do is to get started.' She shot the cuff of her track suit up and looked at her watch. 'It's quarter to seven and the coach leaves at seven-thirty. I need to get breakfast. You don't need to come if it's too early for you.'

Rob fumbled with the buttons on his shirt. 'No, I'll come,' he said. 'I'm supposed to be meeting up with Celia at eight-thirty so I need to get cracking too.'

'I don't know what you're both going to find to do at that time of the morning.'

Rob glanced at her. She had opened the hotel room door and was standing there, bouncing up and down on her heels as if she was on springs. 'Oh, it's a nice morning. We'll go for a walk or something, I expect. OK, I'm ready. Let's go.'

The restaurant was a sea of noisy athletes, barging each other, talking excitedly and cramming food and drink into their mouths. Rob felt that he stuck out like a sore thumb in his good trousers and shirt. He had managed to get them a table, while Kitty had gone to get her food. She was coming back from the counter empty-handed, apart from her own water bottle which seemed to have been glued to her these last few days.

'What's up?' he said, seeing her frown.

'There's no bread for toast and there's no clean dishes and spoons to eat cereals with. Oh, I knew I should have come down earlier.'

'What about that over there?' Rob indicated a counter where he could see steam rising from various trays.

She waved her hand dismissively. 'That's bacon and egg and sausages and other fatty things. You can't run a marathon on that. You'd throw up. Oh damn, what am I going to do? I need to have a belly full of carbs.' She ran her hand through her hair and stared around the room.

'I'll tell you what you're going to do,' said Rob. He picked up a couple of the many used bowls and spoons that littered the dining room. 'Now give us that bottle of water of yours.'

She did as she was told. 'Surely you're not going to... oh Rob, yuk!'

'Well, it's your choice.' He rinsed the used bowl and spoon with

120

water from the bottle, using another bowl to catch the water. 'I'm not in the catering trade for nothing, you know.'

Kitty only hesitated a second before she grabbed the bowl and set off a second time in search of suitable food. She elbowed her way back with a mountain of cornflakes in her bowl, and she was also carrying a stash of bread. 'Some more bread arrived just as I got there. I haven't got time to toast it now.' She set to eating. 'Thank you for the bowl trick,' she mumbled, her mouth full.

'Don't mention it,' said Rob, amused by the whole thing. He would enjoy telling Celia about it later. 'I think I've earned myself a big fry-up now.' He pushed his way through more jostling Marathoners who were just arriving, all of them as disgruntled as Kitty at not having mountains of their precious carbs laid on.

By the time he got back and waded into his plate full of bacon, two eggs, fried bread, baked beans and sausages she was checking her watch again and finishing up the dregs of her cornflakes. 'I'll go back to the room now and fill my water bottle again, then I'll go and get a seat on the coach. I want to be early just in case they've overbooked it.' She took a deep breath and stood up. 'Well, I guess this is it. Wish me luck.'

He put his knife and fork down and stood up with her, holding her lightly by the shoulders. 'You shouldn't need luck with all the hard work you've put in. You just have a great time. Don't let that old man Malcolm slow you down.' Then he hugged her hard.

She sniffed his cheek. 'Mm, is that aftershave? I thought you only got that out for special occasions.'

'My wife's running her first marathon, what's that if not a special occasion? Now off you go and I'll see you later, with your medal.'

He watched as she joined the exodus of runners who were heading for the doors. He let his breath out slowly and forked up some baked beans. Another lucky escape. Whatever was he thinking, putting the aftershave on before she'd gone? But, on the plus side, he was getting to be more able to think on his feet. Like Celia.

*

Kitty stood outside Maze Street station. Was he late? No, it wasn't half-past eight yet. The morning had a slight chill to it, but fine, thank goodness. There she stood in her very own bizarre fashion item, black

121

bin liner with a neck and arm holes torn in it. Some of the runners, like her, were wrapped in bin liners or various other protective and fairly disposable garments. But the majority of the crowd looked very similar in shorts and vests, with their numbers pinned onto them front and back. So many people. She checked her watch again.

'Good morning.' She hadn't seen him approach her through the army of people. He was carrying his bin liner, and he looked especially gangly. Probably it was the shorts. She wasn't used to seeing his arms and long legs.

'Good morning to you. What shall we do today? Do you feel like running a marathon?'

To her relief he matched her manufactured chirpiness with a steady smile. 'I'm not sure I can say that I feel like it, but I'm certainly going to do it.'

'That's the spirit.' She linked her arm with his. 'Just look at all these runners!'

They joined the swarm, following the slow drift of humanity towards the start at Blackheath. They swapped stories about their breakfasts and laughed at their widely different experiences – Kitty's manic one and Malcolm's solitary one.

'We'd better pay a last visit to the toilet,' said Kitty. 'I'll meet you right here, at this tree, in a few minutes.'

She followed the sign to the ladies' toilets and joined the end of a dismayingly enormous queue. The woman who joined just behind her rolled her eyes and said let's hope it moves quickly. It didn't. After ten minutes the queue had hardly budged and Kitty was feeling the effects of all the fluid she had drunk that morning. This is hopeless, another woman remarked, adding that the race would have started before they'd got a chance to pee. Kitty felt her pulse beat rise and her bladder respond even more. Malcolm would be wondering where she was. The complaining around her was gaining momentum, and the fidgeting women were craning their necks to see if the procession was moving any quicker. Oh, blow this for a laugh, came the loud voice of the woman behind to her friend. I'm busting. Come on, let's go over there. She and the friend, both of them having the lightly muscled physiques of seasoned runners, strode off to a nearby tree and started to peel down their shorts. A couple of other women followed, looking around sheepishly. By the time Kitty had worked up the nerve to join them there were more than a dozen women crouched under the tree, with guffaws of laughter covering their embarrassment. Kitty crouched and let go, her eyes carefully glued to the green of the grass in front of her. Oh, the relief! Probably the grass would never be green again after today.

'Sorry to be so long,' she said to Malcolm's rather relieved face. 'There was a long queue.' She opened her mouth to tell him the rest of the story but thought better of it. Time was getting on and they had to get to the start.

*

He felt like a teenager waiting on his first date. He paced up and down on the pavement, the taste of traffic fumes acrid in his mouth, while a steady stream of cars, bikes and black cabs cruised past him. When you lived in a village you just weren't used to this. Across the road two men were lounging on the corner, smoking and chatting, and a couple of scruffy-looking women sauntered by with pushchairs.

Just when he was starting think that their careful plan had gone wrong, that he had given her the wrong street name or something, a taxi slowed down alongside him and Celia emerged. His heart lurched. Even the way she got out of a taxi, sort of unfolding, bewitched him. She looked swish and unruffled in a trim jacket and trousers, with a silky scarf at her throat and her blonde hair neatly combed and pinned up at the back. Even in his shirt and good trousers he felt rumpled and oafish as he stepped forward to meet her.

'You made it, then.' His jacket was slewed across his arm and he passed it onto the other arm. The taxi had started to pull away when it occurred to him that he should have paid for it, and he floundered into an apology, but Celia waved it away.

He groped for the battered map in his jacket pocket. 'The hotel isn't far from here.' He struggled with the unruly paper and tried to fold it to the appropriate part. 'About twenty minutes, I think. Would you be OK to walk?' He glanced anxiously at her shoes, which only had small heels and he thought looked suitable for walking. 'Or we could get a cup of coffee if you like?'

'Perhaps we'll find somewhere to get coffee on the way.' She was smiling as he tried to get the map under control, and she looked around at the buildings, probably out of tact, when his jacket slid off his arm and onto the pavement as he finally wrestled the creased map to the part he wanted.

As they walked through the streets he asked her about the evening with her in-laws, and she in turn asked about his stay in the hotel. They might as well have been acquaintances exchanging polite pleasantries. He had thought they might have held hands while they strolled through the streets. After all, London was swallowing them up and they didn't know anyone. But he didn't dare to reach out for her. Soon they stopped talking because there was just too much traffic noise.

The streets had started to take on a run-down look, with paint peeling and limp plants on doorsteps. He consulted the map. 'I think it's the next turning on the right. Yes, here it is.'

If he had hoped that the hotel he had booked would be determinedly cheerful, a bright spot of colour and class among all the seedy facades, then he was disappointed. He couldn't help but compare it with where he had stayed last night with Kitty, which had been modern, bright and airy. Here they stepped up to a doorway which had a bag of uncollected rubbish on the step. They entered a gloomy hallway where a couple of armchairs sagged and a smell of frying hung in the air. He pressed the bell on the desk and heard its shrill wail reverberating somewhere in the back of the building. He was aware of Celia waiting in perfect stillness next to him. He didn't dare to look at her.

Footsteps down the hallway. A young man with pimples and a brown stain on his dingy white shirt was walking towards them as if he had all the time in the world. 'Can I help you?' he said, without looking at them.

'I made a reservation for last night,' said Rob. 'And I phoned you to say that we wouldn't be here until the morning but we still want the room.'

The young man enquired what name the booking was made in and consulted his ledger. 'Ah, yes. I'm afraid we still have to charge the overnight rate, sir.'

'I realise that. And we would like to keep the room until one o'clock please.'

Celia had melted away to look intently out through the door onto the street, as if something out there was fascinating her. The man looked at Celia and then back at Rob, and grinned, showing some of the worst teeth Rob had ever seen. 'Late check-out is twenty pounds extra, I'm afraid, sir.'

Rob muttered his agreement and finished the payment. The foyer felt hot and stuffy. Why did they have to have it so hot?

'Enjoy your stay, sir,' he said, not even bothering to hide his leer. Rob turned away, gripping the key in his hand. He would have liked to push it down the little turd's throat.

Three floors up and the landing was no more savoury than the ground floor had been. Rob therefore had no great expectations when he opened the door to their attic room. And there it all was. A bed that you just knew was going to be lumpy, a dirt-encrusted window, a limp curtain on a broken rail.

They had climbed up to the room in silence. In fact, Celia had not spoken since they had arrived at the hotel. Now she had put her bag down on the dressing table and was gazing round at the tawdry furnishings. Her face was expressionless.

'Celia, I'm so sorry. You see everything was booked up because of the Marathon. I can't expect you to stay here. Come on, we'll go,' he finished miserably.

Her pale eyes slid onto his. 'No,' she said. 'I want to stay. It's perfect.'

*

'Under four hours, that's what we want,' said Kitty as she scanned the signs of estimated finishing times that were displayed above the path, to find the right place for them to join the queue for the start. A couple of fun runners, a person in a gorilla costume followed by a man in a full tutu and ballet tights, pushed past them. They disappeared into the throng of people, heading further away from the start. It would probably take five or six hours in get-ups like that, she thought.

'I wouldn't fancy running a marathon in some of these costumes, would you?' said Malcolm, as if reading her thoughts. 'It would be

125

incredibly hot and uncomfortable.'

'I suppose a lot of them are planning to have a good time and raise some money for charity, rather than really running it all the way.' Her reply was distracted; she was finding the sheer crowd density and all the bustle and shoving more unnerving than she would have thought. 'Here we are,' she said. '3.45 to four hours. That's us.' She grabbed Malcolm's hand so that they wouldn't get separated and they inserted themselves into the pack of waiting runners. She checked her watch; 9.10.

It was warm in the sea of people and they both peeled off their outer layers. 'Do you think we're in the right place?' said Malcolm in her ear. 'Everybody around us looks like a real runner.'

Kitty knew what he meant. She was glancing sidelong at disconcertingly lean and lithe people, some of whom were jogging lightly on the spot or flexing their shoulders. 'We've been over this,' she said. 'We have to stick to our guns. With the training we've done, we should be good for a sub-four marathon.' She checked her watch again. 9.14. A man wearing a pink curly wig slid in front of her. He smelled strongly of Deep Heat, which didn't seem to go with the wig. She tried to take a step back from to escape the fumes, but she trod on somebody's foot and had to apologise. You didn't need somebody injuring your foot when you were about to run a marathon.

'Not ideal, is it, to be doing all this standing before we set off to run twenty-six point two miles,' she said to Malcolm. Her leg muscles felt like they were tightening up and a grumbling ache was developing in her lower back. 'I just want to get started now.' She glanced at him. He seemed perfectly calm and collected, and that wasn't helping. 'Why are you so serene, anyway? I feel like I'm about to explode.'

He smiled at her, irritatingly. 'Yes, I do feel quite calm, actually. I suppose it's because it's too late to do any more. What will be will be.'

The minutes ticked on. By the time there was two minutes to go, the collective tension in the crowd had swollen to an almost unbearable pitch.

'Kitty, there's something I want to say.'

She was glad of the distraction. 'What is it?'

'I know we'd said that we would run together, the same as in our training, but if I find I have to slow down in the last few miles…'

'You mean the dreaded Wall?'

'Or injury, or anything. Well, if that happens, I want you to go on without me. I won't hold you back. We'll meet up afterwards at the place we agreed on.'

Kitty opened her mouth to tell him, don't be silly, of course they would run together. But then she hesitated. Feeling rather selfish, she said, 'That's very generous of you. But it probably won't be necessary. You can do it.'

And then they heard it. The bang of the starting gun. They knew that Terry Waite had been chosen to fire the gun to start the race, but they were much too far away to catch sight of him. The tension in the crowd of runners was released in a huge cheer. Kitty and Malcom whooped and clapped along with the rest of them.

And then, they waited. And waited. The huge reservoir of pent-up energy seethed. Although Kitty had known it would take ages for the whole procession to squeeze out of the gates of Greenwich Park and actually start running, it still seemed like some of the longest minutes of her life. It took a whole quarter of an hour before her part of the procession eventually picked up their feet and stirred into a sluggish walk. Kitty clicked the start button on her watch. They were underway.

Chapter 11

Ten minutes. Ten minutes gone and they were still basically walking. Several times they had changed gear up into a jog and Kitty had thought, here we go, but a minute later the runners had clogged up again and they were forced to slow down to a sedate shamble.

'I never thought it would be this slow getting going,' said Kitty, not for the first time. 'If we don't start running soon it will really affect our time.'

'When you read the received wisdom about your first marathon they say it doesn't hurt to have slow start. It stops you from shooting off too fast and burning up too much energy in the early stages,' replied Malcolm.

Kitty grunted, but bit back her sharp reply. Since when was he such an expert? It's me who's done all the reading. Well, most of it. And how come he was so relaxed? She looked around at her fellow runners. On the whole they seemed to be in a jolly mood, either chatting and smiling, or else looking calm and focussed. Why weren't they looking as frustrated as she felt?

Malcolm, on the other hand, was quite glad of the gentle start. He was conscious of his muscles warming up nicely and he felt himself, both mentally and physically, bed into his place in this carnival of runners. They were situated close to the right-hand side of the road. Just in front of him were two women dressed identically in schoolgirl outfits, gymslips, black stockings, straw boaters, the lot. They were waving enthusiastically at the few onlookers who had turned out to give the runners a good luck cheer to start them on their way. By his right-hand side, between him and the pavement, was someone who Malcolm had ascertained from a couple of glances to be a short podgy man with a bandage round his knee. He seemed to give a slight whistle every time he breathed. There were certainly all shapes and sizes in this Marathon. And then, by his left-hand side there was Kitty, exuding stress and nervousness with every step. Poor Kitty. Despite all her brave talk, she had not yet learned to be patient rather than struggle.

'I didn't expect any supporters out here near the start, did you?' he said. He waved and smiled tentatively at a couple of lipsticked girls on the side-lines and, to his embarrassed surprise, he was rewarded by kisses blown to him.

Kitty didn't reply. Then she said, 'Look,' indicating ahead to the curve of balloons hung over the road, with the number one embedded in the middle, 'We're just coming up to the first mile marker and all we're doing is jogging.' Suddenly they were brought up short as people stopped in front of them at the sight of the first drinks station. There was confusion; runners were abruptly veering across to the roadside tables set out with cups of water where cheery volunteers rushed to slosh out more. Kitty hesitated, thinking of the wisdom that had been drummed into her by everything that she had read about marathon running: *drink at every opportunity. Drink, drink, drink...* 'We haven't exactly expended much effort yet,' she said to Malcolm. 'Let's miss out this drinks station.'

Malcolm was also mindful of the *drink, drink, drink* mantra but he didn't think it was worth arguing, with Kitty in this mood. She was probably right anyway. They crunched their way over dropped plastic cups, like seashells on a beach. The crowd had thinned after the hiatus of the drinks station, with many runners pausing to gulp their cupful.

'At last,' said Kitty. 'Let's see if we can make some time up, now that we've got a bit of space.' She accelerated and began to weave around slower runners. Malcolm tagged along in her wake.

'Do you think this is worth it?' he said after a few minutes of frantic swerving. 'We're using a lot of energy breaking our rhythm like this. And we don't want to pull any muscles with all this sideways movement.'

'Malcolm, it took us eleven minutes to cover that first mile. I've come here to run this damn Marathon, not to walk it. If you don't want to do it together then fine, I'll see you at the end.'

*

129

Rob hovered by the door as Celia took her jacket off and folded it over the back of the chair. She slipped her shoes off and placed them under it, paired neatly side by side. Then she sat down on the bed and swung her legs up onto it. It creaked. Of course it creaked.

'I don't understand,' he said, still not moving from near the door. 'What do you mean, it's perfect?' He gestured around him. 'It's hardly that.'

She unknotted the silky scarf from around her neck. 'Of course I wouldn't want to be here normally, and especially not to spend the night here. But for an illicit tryst such as ours, it sets the scene perfectly. That's all I meant.'

Rob shifted from one foot to the other as he tried to catch up with what was happening. He had wanted to impress her, to take her somewhere within his limited means that was comfortable and tasteful. That certainly wasn't this place and yet she seemed happy with it. An illicit tryst, she had said. The memory of his mother saying that Celia wanted a bit of rough slid into his mind, and he quickly supressed the thought.

She laid her hand on the bed next to her and for the first time since arriving she smiled slightly. 'Aren't you coming to join me?'

*

Kitty had regretted the words as soon as they were out of her mouth. And Malcolm not saying anything but gamely sticking alongside her only made her feel worse. After a few minutes her guilt built up enough for her to say, 'I'm sorry; that was uncalled for. Of course I would prefer for us to run together. It's just that my body's craving to get on with it after all those weeks of training. I so much want to do the best time I possibly can. Definitely under four hours.' Nevertheless she moderated the swerving manoeuvres around other runners. She glanced across at Malcolm and he smiled his patient smile at her.

'It's OK,' he said. 'I know you want to do your best and I know you're very worked up. I think the crowd is definitely evening itself out now, though. This is pretty much our normal pace, I would think.'

Yet another Lycra-clad man cut across in front of them with a muttered 'excuse me' and rushed up to a nearby wall to have a pee in what passed for semi-privacy. This had been happening since the beginning of the race, which amazed Kitty. Surely these men had gone to the toilet before they started? She thought that Malcolm must have noticed it too, but she didn't mention it.

At the fifth mile marker they skimmed past the drinks station and swooped up their cups of water, slowing to a jog to swallow them. 'We've got this drinking technique perfected now,' said Kitty. 'We hardly have to slow down at all.'

'And we don't spill any,' said Malcolm, discarding his cup and trying to burp quietly. 'I'd say that was quite an accomplishment.'

But Kitty hadn't heard because she was poring over her watch with a frown of concentration. 'We did those last two miles at well under an eight minute mile pace. Good. If we can keep going a bit faster, like this, we'll more than make the time up.'

Malcolm didn't reply. He wondered if he should voice his misgivings, namely that going too fast in the first half of a marathon was considered one of the worst things you could do, and also everyone else was in the same boat about having an enforced slow start. He could quite clearly see in his mind's eye the page from the book that Adela had bought him: *Don't be tempted to go too fast in the first half. Aim to keep your pace even throughout.* And there had been an illustration on the same page of a grizzled elderly runner, bone-thin and grimly determined, slogging along a highway somewhere. It had stuck in his mind, for some reason.

But he didn't like to nag Kitty now that she had settled down and seemed to be enjoying herself. As ever, her bright mood infected him and they interspersed silent stretches with swapped low-voiced asides about their fellow runners, the undulating sea of Lycra, colours, sweat bands, knee supports. She was happy and therefore so was he.

There was another reason why he didn't want to suggest that they slow down, and he allowed himself to visit the shadowy corner of his mind where his thoughts were masquerading as consideration for Kitty. In truth, despite what he had said to her as they waited at the start line, he didn't want her to go off on her own and leave him to cope. He had always relied on her to motivate him and keep him going with her chirpy, straightforward company.

He didn't want to be alone with his thoughts, alone in this vast sea

131

of people.

*

They lay side by side underneath the coverlet and Rob felt his breathing gradually return to normal.

'That was great,' he said, his hand caressing her thigh. 'You seemed... different.'

'How so?'

Rob thought about it while he looked at the naked light bulb above them. How had she been different? Normally she was quite shy, reticent even. She today she had been more... brazen. As if she was playing the tart. He wasn't sure that he liked the change.

Deciding that he couldn't say any of that, he replied 'You seemed more confident today. You knew what you wanted.'

She lay still beside him. 'It's different being out of my own home. There's always a feeling of restraint there.'

'Yes, I can see that. Oh, and there was that time when your daughter came home unexpectedly. Do you remember? God, that was close. You saved the day by pretending I was a workman. You did it so convincingly too.'

'Mm... I did, didn't I.' Rob recalled how easily she had become the Lady of the Manor and him the servant.

Footsteps sounded in the corridor and paused outside their room. The knock on the door was a waste of time because it was followed straightaway by the handle turning and a young brown-skinned woman staring at them, her arms laden with towels. There was a second's suspended pause before she backed out, murmuring something that Rob didn't catch. Her face hadn't expressed any emotion, only weariness.

'My God,' said Rob, leaning his head back on the pillow, feeling his pulse pounding. 'What a shock. I'm glad she didn't come in ten minutes earlier.'

Celia seemed altogether unperturbed by the incident. 'I imagine in her job she's seen everything,' she said. 'But perhaps we should lock the door.'

She's a cool customer, thought Rob, with admiration.

*

132

'There it is,' said Kitty. 'Can you see it?' She pointed ahead to the giant skeletal frame, like a winter tree reaching out its branches to sweep the sky. 'It's even more impressive than in pictures.'

'Oh yes,' replied Malcolm. 'The Cutty Sark. The world's sole-surviving tea clipper and the fastest and greatest of her time, so it's said. She certainly is magnificent.' The sun was shining now, and the background of blue sky showed the ship off to perfection.

'And the crowd,' said Kitty. 'Just look how many people there are!' From a sprinkling of supporters along the kerbsides, the crowd had swelled fourfold and an undulation of cheering and clapping burst in on them. Kitty felt herself lifted on the tide of goodwill, and she waved back enthusiastically. Hands reached over the barriers, some holding out sweets for the runners. She caught the eye of one elderly man as she sailed past. 'Good on yer, love,' he called out to her. 'Wish I could do it.' There was no chance to reply as she and Malcolm surged onwards.

Now they were coming right alongside the Cutty Sark itself. Kitty craned her neck to see up to the top. You could really tell how big and impressive it was now. Rob and I will have to bring Danny to London to see all these sights, she thought. At the prow of the ship the road bent itself right around in a hairpin so that now they were running along the other side of the Cutty Sark. There was music wafting in the air from a jazz band that was in full swing outside a pub. Now the crowd, who were obviously having a good time, had plastic pint glasses of lager in their hands and were offering swigs of beer to the runners rather than sweets.

'Imagine drinking beer at this time on a Sunday morning,' said Malcolm.

'A great opportunity to make some money, though,' said Kitty. 'Rob would really get his teeth into this. He'd lay on themed cocktails, special snacks, the lot. He does it when a cycle race comes past us.'

'That's six and a half miles, isn't it?' said Malcolm as the noise and the partying crowds dwindled. 'We're a quarter of the way through already.'

'That's right.' She laughed. 'You see it on TV, but that was even better than I imagined. The great London Marathon party.'

Malcolm had been affected by the party atmosphere too. For those

133

few mad moments around the Cutty Sark he hadn't thought about the hard slog ahead; he had just enjoyed what was happening around him. But now it was time to focus again.

'Let's dig in and get some solid miles in through the docks and up to the halfway mark at Tower Bridge,' Kitty said, as if she was reading his mind. 'I've never seen the bridge before, like I hadn't seen Cutty Sark. In fact, I've hardly ever been to London. Oh Malcolm, this is great. And perfect weather for running. Everything's on our side now.'

They settled down and sucked up the quieter miles. The noise of hundreds of feet on tarmac accompanied them and drummed a steady, hypnotising rhythm. The fun runners in fancy dress that they had seen at the beginning of the race had largely been left behind and now they were part of a body of runners that was fairly uniform in shorts and singlets, moving ever forward like a column of ants. Whereas on their training runs Kitty and Malcolm used to chatter pretty much non-stop, now they didn't feel inclined to hold much of a conversation as they focussed and let their bodies do the work.

The river Thames opened up on each side of them as they mounted onto Tower Bridge.

'You said you've never seen it before?' asked Malcolm.

'No,' said Kitty, too busy looking round her at the impressive structure to say more. Like at Cutty Sark, the supporting crowd billowed around them uproariously. What with that and the blue sky, she felt like she was flying.

'I have seen it, but from the river bank, never on the bridge itself,' said Malcolm. He remembered a time a few years ago when they had come as a family to London for a weekend break. After doing Buckingham Palace and Big Ben they had split up. Celia had gone shopping with Adela while he and David had gone to the Tower of London. There had been a conspiratorial air between them as they escaped from the women and set off to view, with proper manly interest, the weaponry and historical artefacts. David would have been, what, about thirteen, just hovering between childhood and adolescence. Malcolm himself had politely gazed at suits of armour, swords and shields. David, on the other hand, had been fascinated and had asked Malcolm enthusiastic questions, most of which he had had to fudge in order to come up with any sort of answer. There had been a sizeable queue to see the Crown Jewels so they had skipped that and instead gone for a walk. That's what had triggered his memory: the two of them standing on the riverside looking up at the bridge. David had hoped that it would open, but of course it didn't. They had been eating gigantic ice creams, which had been scaled down in size when they later told Celia about their morning. It had only taken the ice cream for David to step back into boyhood, and he had devoured it with great gusto, getting a fleck of ice cream on his nose in the process. *Why on earth am I remembering an inconsequential thing like that?*

'The half way mark,' said Kitty, and she joined in with the other runners' clapping and cheering. She glanced at Malcolm's pensive face. 'Are you OK?'

He roused himself. 'Yes. Yes, of course. I was just lost in a memory about a previous time that I had been in London.' She asked what the memory was about, and so he told her.

'You don't often talk about your son now.'

'That's because it's a lot better than it used to be. You've helped enormously with that, Kitty. You're the only person that I feel I can talk to about how I feel.'

'Celia and you still don't talk about David much, then?'

'No.'

Kitty waited. When he didn't say more, she added, 'I wonder what they're doing now? Rob and Celia, that is. Rob didn't seem to have anything in mind. Did Celia?'

'I didn't ask. Well, it's a lovely day. Perhaps they've gone for a walk. Or found somewhere to watch the Marathon for a while.'

'Perhaps.' The truth was she wasn't really that interested. Rob, the pub, even Danny, her whole life, seemed remote at present. The only thing that existed was now, this very moment, this succession of moments where she lived simply to put one foot in front of the other and to keep on doing that for as long as it took. She had waited all her life for this.

*

Here it is, thought Rob. *I knew I saw a café along here somewhere.* It wasn't busy inside. There was a table of four old guys, who looked as

135

though they were making their teas last as long as possible, and that was it. They reminded him of some of his old guys, sitting in the corner of the Bar and eking their beer out. The man behind the counter was sitting on a stool reading the paper. He put it down and smiled cheerfully at Rob.

'Alright, mate? What can I get yer?'

'Can you do me a tea and a coffee to take away, please mate?'

'Coming up.' Hot water hissed down a spout and he spooned instant coffee into a large paper cup. 'Nice day for the race,' he added.

'What? Oh yes, the Marathon.'

'Probably getting a bit too hot for them runners, though. They like it cool and cloudy.'

Rob agreed. Then he added, 'My wife's running in it. It's her first time.'

The man added milk to both drinks. 'You don't say? Well, good for her. My missus couldn't run to the end of the street.'

Rob carried the drinks back carefully along the street with the sun warm on his back. He had biscuits tucked inside his jacket pocket. He had wondered whether to get a couple of nice looking Danish pastries that he had seen there, but he thought they might end up all squashed inside his pockets. He looked up at the hotel, at the windows on the top floor. In one of those rooms Celia was waiting for him. He wondered how Kitty was doing.

*

'I didn't think it would get this hot,' said Malcolm. He brushed the sweat out of his eyes, yet again, with his wristband.

'I hope we're drinking enough to stay hydrated,' said Kitty. 'Perhaps we should take two cups of water at the next drinks station. This is certainly the hottest weather we've run in.' There was a First Aid station by the roadside, and several people were sitting there with their shoes and socks peeled off while patient volunteers dabbed at their feet. One man was writhing with the agonies of cramp in his calf. It's getting serious now, thought Kitty. 'Are you still feeling OK?' she asked Malcolm. 'No blisters or anything?'

'I'm feeling surprisingly OK,' said Malcolm. 'Better than I thought I would. Our training regime – or should I say your regime, because you planned it all - is paying off. Of course, my body knows that it's already run eighteen miles, but there's plenty left in the old legs yet.'

'I'm feeling alright too. And we're nearly half an hour ahead of these guys.' She nodded at the runners coming up the other side of the road where, for the first time, the Marathon course had looped back on itself for a stretch. 'Gosh, we're definitely doing better than them. Look, some are even walking already. Even though we're sure to slow down in the last few miles, I hope we can finish it without much walking,' she said.

'They're doing their best,' said Malcolm, amused at how derisive she was.

'I didn't mean they weren't. They've probably trained less than us, and are not aiming for a sub-four like we are. That is, four hours not counting the fifteen minutes it took us to get to the starting line, of course.'

'Anyway, it's nice to see the fronts of runners rather than only the backs of those who are ahead of us.' After studying them more Malcolm added, 'I notice that some of them seem to be having these gel drinks, or eating something. I thought eating while you run wasn't supposed to be a good idea.'

'I don't really know if it helps or not. We didn't do it in training. And do you remember I told you that when I trained for a half marathon last year I tried eating on the run and it made me feel really sick? But maybe we could try it next time.'

'Next time?'

'Of course. This is so brilliant you couldn't only do it once.'

He didn't reply straight away because they were approaching the twenty mile drinks station and paused to collect their water and swallow it down. Malcolm poured a second cupful over his head and gratefully felt the coolness run down his chest and back.

'Twenty miles,' he said. 'We're heading into unknown territory now. What do they say? *Twenty miles is only half way.* And Kitty, please let's not think about any next time. This one isn't safely in the bag yet.'

*

She was still lying in bed when he got back with the drinks, the cover pulled up to her shoulders, just as he had left her.

'I hope you weren't worried,' he said. 'It was a bit further to the café than I remembered.' There was no bedside table, so he stood holding both cups, unsure where to put them down.

'No, I was dozing, in fact,' she said. 'I never sleep very well when we're staying at my brother-in-law's house.' She sat up in bed. He watched the swing of her breasts as she reached onto the floor for her blouse. She put the blouse on, but not her bra, and left the buttons half undone. She reached down to the floor again for her pants. He only saw a flash of pale pink before she had pulled them into bed and was putting them on under the covers.

Rob swallowed and laughed nervously. 'Is this a sort of reverse striptease?' he said. 'If so, it's having the right effect. And I don't mean a reverse effect.'

She looked at him in surprise. 'I was only getting a bit decent so that I could come and sit in the chair to drink my coffee.'

So it seemed that the raunchy role she had played was over, and the half-shy, rather prim woman he was used to was back. On the whole he was glad.

She got out of bed and sat in the chair. He put the coffee down on the dressing table beside her and revealed the biscuits that he had brought for her, placing them beside the cup like an offering. Because there was nowhere else to sit, he perched awkwardly on the side of the bed with his tea. Outside, traffic droned endlessly even though it was Sunday.

She nibbled at a shortcake biscuit. A few crumbs dropped down onto her cleavage where she had hadn't done her blouse up, but she didn't seem to notice. Rob could see the outline of her nipples through the thin fabric of the blouse. He gulped at his tea and then gasped because it was hot. She crossed her legs. Her pants were plain and reached all the way up to her waist. They were nothing like as fancy or brief as what Kitty wore, yet he thought he had never seen anything more sexy than the way they smoothed all over her rounded belly. He glanced at his watch. Yes, there was time. Plenty of time.

*

It was after the twenty-first mile that they started to see real marathon casualties. Malcolm was aware of a certain grimness that had started to descend on the runners, and the average pace had definitely slowed. More and more people were resorting to a stiff walk for a while before picking up again to a pained jog. So far he and Kitty had managed to keep jogging along. A man a few feet in front of them was weaving drunkenly as he stumbled along, and suddenly he doubled up and vomited over the road. Someone from the crowd leant out to offer him tissues and water.

'Poor chap,' said Malcom as they veered round him.

Kitty didn't reply. Malcolm glanced at her. Sweat was standing out on her brow and her face was blank.

'Kitty? Are you alright?'

She frowned. 'Not really. Suddenly I feel awful.' She shook her head as if to clear her vision. 'I was fine half a mile ago. Tired, you know, but coping. But now... I feel like all my energy has gone.'

He kept his voice light. 'There's only just over four miles to go now. You can do that. We knew it was going to be tough in the last section.'

'I've got to slow down,' she said. 'My legs just won't keep going.' She slowed to a wobbly walk.

'That's fine. It doesn't matter if we walk for a bit. I could do with slowing down, anyway.'

She hobbled along with Malcolm beside her. He looked ahead, straining to see the twenty-two mile drinks station. There it was.

'We're coming to a drinks station,' he said. That will do you good. Look, there it is.'

When they got there she took her water obediently and drank it down. She blinked at Malcolm as if she hardly recognised him. 'What's happening? It was all going so well...' she trailed off in confusion.

It was textbook. 'This is what we read about,' he said. 'It's the Wall. Classic symptoms, I'd say.'

She stumbled on, while some runners overtook them. They were going past the Tower of London and Tower Bridge, where less than a couple of hours ago they had been so jubilant as they ran over it. She gazed at the bridge, unable to marshal her thoughts, and she was puzzled by the memory of herself running like a gazelle across it just that short time ago. All she wanted to do now was to stop and not have to churn her legs round any more. The thought of lying down on the pavement was blissful. But no, the dim voice in the back of her head told her that she had to finish this marathon. So she had to keep going. She just didn't know how.

'Just think about getting to the next mile marker for now, that's all. You can do that, can't you Kitty?'

She could, but it was slow, painfully slow. Kitty had to make a huge effort to instruct her body to move. She felt like a baby learning to walk. Everything, even thinking, was hard work. She plugged on for the next ten minutes. 'Why isn't this happening to you?' she said to Malcolm.

'I honestly don't know. I expect everyone's metabolism is different. I'm tired, but not like you, you poor thing. But Kitty, you *can* make it. You've worked so hard for this. *You can do it.*'

He said it with more conviction than he felt. Her glassy stare and how quickly she had run out of steam were alarming him.

'And I thought I could do a sub-four marathon.'

He took her hand. 'It doesn't matter. Just getting there is enough.'

Her hand was inert in his. 'You go on without me,' she said dully. 'You could still do sub-four.'

He tightened his grip on her hand. 'I wouldn't dream of it. I'll look after you. Look, the twenty-three mile drinks station is coming up. Just focus on that for now.'

She limped up and accepted her drink, then set off again at a pace that was a mere dragging walk now. Malcolm cast around in his mind for how to keep her going.

'Kitty, what would you do now if your home was on fire and Danny was trapped inside and you had to run to a phone box to phone the fire brigade? You'd find the energy to run then, wouldn't you?'

The trick had got through to her, and she picked up her pace a fraction. Malcolm watched her anxiously. He himself was very weary, but not like this. Besides which, all his effort now was focussed on her and his own fatigue he felt only dimly.

They entered into the gloom of a short tunnel, which gave them some welcome shade. When they came out into the bright daylight again, suddenly there was a multitude of spectators and they were enveloped by a gigantic roaring cheer from them. Kitty felt the power

140

of the sudden noise and light like a physical blow and total disorientation overtook her. In her confusion, it felt like a threat and her brain refused to cope. She stumbled and might have fallen if Malcolm hadn't been there to steady her. She floundered towards the side of the road and sat down, clasping her head in her hands.

'I can't do it,' she whispered. 'I can't go on any more.'

*

Celia was sitting on the bed fully dressed and putting lipstick on when Rob emerged from the bathroom after coaxing the sulky shower into life.

'Where would you like to go to lunch?' he said. 'Go on, name it. Anywhere you want.' He unwrapped the towel from his waist and vigorously dried his back. He was glowing, invigorated, king of the world. Sex twice in a morning and a nearly cold shower will do it every time, he thought.

She didn't look at him but took a comb out of her bag and started to tidy her hair. He watched her as he pulled his trousers on. 'Beautiful hair you've got,' he said. 'I remember that from the first time you came into the pub. You came and had lunch on your own, do you remember? You looked like some sort of angel. And you brought photographs of your Dad and his motorbike. We'll have to go out on the bike again soon.'

She smiled faintly. He wasn't sure if it was for the compliment about her hair or the memory of lunch in the pub. 'I don't know anywhere around here,' she said. 'Perhaps we should go back to near where we're meeting Malcolm and Kitty.'

'Whatever you want,' he said, pulling his shirt on. It was a bit crumpled from where he'd tossed it anyhow on the floor. Suddenly he paused and said, 'Do you ever think about what might happen if we got found out?'

'No,' she said. 'I don't think about anything much nowadays.'

*

Malcolm sat down next to Kitty and silently put his arm round her while she cried softly, hunched up on the kerbside with her knees drawn up to her chest. A sea of runners' legs cruised past at eye level. None of the runners spoke to them or even noticed them, it seemed.

141

They were all too engrossed in their own personal battles.

'My dear,' said Malcolm, 'take a little rest and then you'll be able to keep going. It's only half a mile to the twenty-four mile marker. Just think about getting to there.' He spoke as soothingly as he could, but in truth he was desperate to know what to do to help her. Although he knew what *not* to do, and that was to voice his suspicion that Kitty hitting the Wall so badly was in part due to going too fast in the early stages of the marathon. However, what was done was done.

'Here you are, get this down you.' The voice came from a man in the crowd who had crouched down beside them. He was middle-aged, stout and ruddy, with a magnificently wayward beard, rather like an out-of-season Santa Claus. He thrust a Mars Bar at Kitty while his eyes met Malcolm's in sympathy.

Kitty shook her head. 'Thank you, but I think I'd be sick,' she said.

'Nah, best thing in the world, chocolate, when you need a lift,' he said. 'And anyway, if you are sick, it tastes almost as good coming up as going down,' he added gleefully.

Kitty hesitated. Malcolm decisively took the Mars Bar and thanked the man, who patted Kitty on the shoulder and wished them good luck before he lumbered to his feet and melted back into the crowd. As if not to be outdone, a woman appeared at their other side and pressed a packet of jelly-babies on them. Malcolm thought that he had never experienced such goodwill.

Malcolm unwrapped the chocolate and broke some off for Kitty. 'You heard the man,' he said. 'Now come on, eat.'

To his relief she responded to his insistence and ate the entire bar. Then he pulled her to her feet and guided her back gently into the stream of runners. Malcolm was surprised how much he had stiffened up from that rest, short as it was, and both he and Kitty were hobbling along at a medium walking pace. He watched her anxiously as they drank their water at the twenty four mile station. She wiped her arm across her mouth after throwing her empty cup away. She looked at Malcolm and he could have cried with relief as he saw the old Kitty coming back.

'I feel a bit better now,' she said.

*

'That was a good meal,' said Rob, putting his knife and fork down onto the gravy remaining on his plate.

'As good as at *The Spinning Coins*?' said Celia.

'Oh, I wouldn't go that far.' He liked her in this mood; light and teasing. He didn't feel so out of his depth. Perhaps it was the place, too. They had eventually decided to go to a nearby pub, because Celia said that it might be too crowded right in the city centre near the end of the Marathon, where they had arranged to meet Malcolm and Kitty. They could get a taxi afterwards. Rob wasn't used to all this getting taxis business. It made him feel swanky, as did having Celia sitting opposite him. He had been aware of glances at their table, people trying to assess them. If Celia had been in another mood, it might have made him feel awkward. But as it was he sat back and lapped it all up. Let them wonder.

The TV was on in the pub, above Celia's head, showing the Marathon. The camera was following the lead runners. Rob wasn't watching it, but he couldn't help be distracted a bit by the images, especially when the camera switched from the lead runners to the main mass of ordinary runners. This is exactly why I don't have TV in my pub, he thought. It's hard not to watch it.

Rob dragged his eyes away from the screen and checked on the time. 'Kitty was pretty sure they were going to finish the Marathon in less than four hours,' he said. 'Then apparently there would be some waiting around time at the start and the finish to add to the total time. So how about some pudding? Coffee? A brandy on the side? Anything you fancy.'

She looked at her watch too. 'Yes, there's still time. Shall we look at the dessert menu?'

Celia picked up her menu when it came. Rob left his unopened on the table. He cleared his throat and leaned across the table to her. 'I've been wondering. When do you think we can meet next? Danny's on Easter holidays from now so for a couple of weeks it won't be so easy.'

She lifted her eyes and looked at him across the top of the menu. 'And Malcolm is taking time off work between now and Easter to recover from the Marathon, he says. It seems like we'll have to leave it until your son goes back to school.'

'It seems a pity,' he said, trying not to sound dejected that her eagerness didn't match his. 'After this morning.'

She pointed to the menu, dismissing the subject. She started to tell him what she wanted, but he didn't hear what she said, because his eye had been caught by the scene of the crowd of Marathoners on the TV screen.

The great human mass was streaming past, mainly quite slowly. The image was gone before he could be totally sure, but he would almost have put money on it that he saw Kitty gamely shuffling along, with Malcolm at her side.

*

They walked a bit, jogged a bit, all along the Embankment. They pressed on doggedly with the great River Thames flowing reassuringly on their left hand side. Kitty felt like she had awoken from a nightmare, although she was still desperately tired, and there wasn't a bit of her that didn't ache. Aching legs she had expected, but not this all-pervading fatigue down into her very bones, that extended from her neck right down to her feet. Yet her brain was more or less functioning again, thank goodness. That scary time where bewilderment had taken over was receding. And the crowd! She was once again in a place where she could appreciate the colossal wave of support that came from these people.

At the twenty-five mile marker Malcolm tore open the pack of jelly-babies and offered her one. She shook her head. 'You need some too,' she said. Malcolm hesitated. Whereas he hadn't experienced the Wall like Kitty, he certainly felt as if he could do with a boost. 'After all,' she added, 'Who'll look after me if you keel over?'

That persuaded him, even though he knew it was deliberate on her part. They ate the jelly-babies between them, gobbling them down one after the other.

'Gosh, that hit the spot,' he said. 'I haven't eaten jelly-babies since I was a boy. The red ones were my favourite, as I recall. But right now I didn't care what colour they were.'

They were turning onto the Mall, wide and straight, with Buckingham Palace to greet them at the bottom of the road. They were shuffling along at the slowest of slow jogs, like many of the runners,

144

although there were some who were barely able to walk. You get used to it, thought Malcolm, and they skirted around someone who had stopped in front of them and was doubled over, trying to ease whatever pain it was that had assailed him – cramp, probably. It's not that you don't care, it's more that you've become desensitised to all the endeavour and suffering around you; desensitised because it just goes on and on, and because you have your work cut out just keeping your own self together.

Keep right on to the end of the road... Kitty sang the words in her head over and over, blocking out everything else, hypnotising herself. It was dulling the enormous fatigue in her body and also it was stopping her from looking at her watch. She had visualised this moment in training, a triumphant but weary last surge down the Mall, and then turning the corner to see Big Ben looming in front of her. She had so hoped, calculated, and expected really, that she would finish comfortably within four hours. But instead she had all but collapsed and was struggling even to complete the distance. The crowd were going mad around them, and a few runners were dredging up their last bit of their energy to put on a bit more speed to cross the finishing line.

'We're almost there.' Malcolm's voice sounded funny and she looked at him, seeing that he was almost crying. The finishing line was just ahead of them with the clock overhead announcing the elapsed time. Kitty didn't allow herself to look at it. Instead she felt for Malcolm's hand and they crossed the line together. Someone was putting a medal around their necks and exhorting them to keep moving. They were herded along within the conveyor belt of runners towards where they would collect their crinkly blue and silver metal blankets. When they were out of the finishing funnel Malcolm put his arms around Kitty and hugged her. Even to raise her arms up around his neck was an effort. She understood why he didn't say anything.

Only then did she look at her watch. After allowing for the fifteen minutes it had taken before they had crossed the start line, Malcom and Kitty had completed the 1992 London Marathon in four hours nine minutes.

Chapter 12

Rob pulled on pink rubber gloves and poured bleach into both toilets in the Ladies' room. Then he washed the floor with a mop and bucket of hot soapy water, backing his way out through the door as he did so. He inspected the mirrors for finger marks and decided that they would do. Whoever thought running a pub was glamorous was wrong, he thought.

Danny was sitting at the kitchen table playing with half a dozen Dinky cars. He was leaning over the table, his head close to the surface, making low revving noises as he manoeuvred the traffic along roads that were only visible to him. 'Alright, champ?' Rob said as he passed through the kitchen and pushed the back door open, to empty the grey water from the bucket down the drain. 'How about some toast for breakfast, then?' he added when he came back in. 'I'm ready for a break.'

Without taking his eyes off the cars Danny said, 'When's Mum getting up? Can I go and see her?'

Rob stripped off the gloves and flexed his hands. They always got sweaty inside rubber gloves. 'Better not. We said we'd leave Mum to rest, didn't we, because she made such a big effort yesterday in the Marathon so now she's very tired.'

'And she was on TV.'

'So she was. Your Mum's famous now.'

'Can I see her on TV?'

'A bit later. I've got to finish this cleaning first.' He ejected two pieces of toast from the toaster. 'And she's only on TV for a minute, mind.' Kitty had set up the video to record the whole race, so last evening he and Kitty had sat on the sofa while he had trawled through the recording around the time that they reckoned the clip would be.

And sure enough, there she was, trotting along with the rest. 'Look, it's you!' he had said triumphantly, pointing at the screen. 'I said it was you.' Kitty had smiled wanly. She was exhausted, poor love. He had tried to persuade her that it was a great achievement, she was his brave girl, and what did it matter if she had been a few minutes slower than she'd hoped. She'd never done it before, after all. She had nodded and thanked him, but he could see she was still disappointed. A good night's sleep is what you need, he had told her.

'Why have you got to do the cleaning?' said Danny. 'That's what Maisie does.'

'Maisie's gone on her holidays,' said Rob. 'And the other person who's supposed to be our cleaner phoned me this morning to say she can't come because she's poorly.' Rob had leapt out of bed at seven o'clock to get the phone before its shrill ring woke Kitty, to hear the whining voice of Sharon, who came in when Maisie had time off, complaining of a stomach upset. He nudged Danny. 'You could help me though.'

Danny wrinkled his nose up and shook his head, brightening as Rob put two slices of buttered toast in front of him. Rob left him messily spooning jam onto his toast, while he got out the vacuum cleaner and headed into the Lounge. The last couple of glasses from the previous night were lingering on a table. Doris had just come in, hair in curlers, and was picking the glasses up to put them on the bar.

Rob put the vacuum cleaner down and greeted his mother. This was the first time they had been alone together since she had read the riot act about Celia, and he had told her that he would do as he pleased. He squirmed inwardly at the memory, which neither of them had mentioned since. They had been polite enough to each other when other people were around, and perhaps only he had been aware of a certain chill.

'What's all this?' she said, indicating the vacuum cleaner. 'Where's that girl?'

'She phoned in sick first thing this morning. Stomach upset.'

Doris snorted. 'Stomach upset, my arse. Hangover, more like. Me and your Dad only ever used to have older cleaners, not these flighty young girls. You can't rely on them.'

147

Rob could have written the script. 'You know how hard it is to get any sort of cleaner,' he said over his shoulder as he lifted stools upside-down onto tables. 'And Sharon hasn't let us down before. Well, only once or twice anyway.'

'And where's Kitty? She usually pitches in if she has to.'

'I've left her to lie in a bit. She was so tired last night.' Doris made a noise that could have meant anything. Rob pressed on. 'I told you when we came back how well she did. There's even a clip of her on TV. Lucky I recorded it. I thought of showing it to you yesterday but by the time I found it, it was past nine o'clock and a bit late to go knocking on your door.'

'You could have knocked all you wanted. I wasn't there.'

She turned round and marched out. Rob sighed and turned the vacuum cleaner on. Danny went skipping through the Lounge with jam down his clean tee shirt, which Rob chose to ignore. He was just getting into the swing of things when Doris came back and tapped him on the shoulder, indicating that he should turn the machine off.

'Come on, I'll do that,' she said. 'I've fetched my overall.' She pulled it on over her head.

'You don't have to,' he said, without much conviction. 'I can do it.'

She shook her head and took the cleaner from him. 'You'll only do half a job.'

Before she could switch it back on he put his hand over hers. 'Ma...'

She looked at him cautiously. 'What now?'

'I just wanted to say... to say I'm sorry about that argument we had the other day. I mean, you're entitled to your view and I shouldn't have said those things and I certainly shouldn't have shouted at you like that.'

'I only said what I thought. I've only ever wanted what's best for you.'

He dropped his eyes from hers. 'I know,' he said. She hadn't removed her hand and he squeezed it. 'Are you sure you don't mind doing this vacuuming? You're one in a million, you are.' Please, not another lecture, he thought. Or, even worse, is she going to ask me if I saw Celia yesterday.'

'Mum, Granny,' shouted Danny, running in from the bottom of the

148

stairs. 'Mum can't walk down the stairs! She's had to turn round and come down backwards just like a baby. Come and see! She looks so funny!'

*

He answered on the third ring. 'Hello Malcolm? How are you feeling?' said Kitty into the phone.

'Tired, but that's not surprising. How are you?' His voice sounded muffled.

'Same. But yesterday when I first got out of bed – oh my God! My legs were unbelievably stiff and sore! I even had to come downstairs backwards. They eased up during the day and are getting back to normal now. Were you like that?'

'Not as bad as you're describing, but yes, my legs were pretty sore too.'

Kitty sat back on the sofa and curled her legs under her in her favourite telephone position, the one she used when she was gossiping with Tina. Immediately her thighs groaned at her so she uncurled her legs and sat normally. 'So, did you have a good long rest yesterday? You were taking this week off work, weren't you?' Either he didn't reply, or she didn't hear him. 'Malcolm? Are you there?'

'Yes, sorry. Yes, I'm starting to recuperate.'

When he didn't say anymore, she said, 'What are you going to do for the rest of the week? Do you think we should try to have a run? They say it's good to have just a short jog a few days after a marathon, to help recovery.'

'I don't think I could run a step today.'

'Me neither. But how about in a couple of days' time? Say Thursday? Just short one,' she added.

'Yes. Yes, Thursday would be OK. And I'd like to see you.'

'And I'd really like to see you too. I keep going over it in my head. If only I'd gone slower in those first few miles.' She sighed. 'Well, everyone else seems pleased for me so I suppose I'll have to be pleased too. Oh, and Malcolm, did you see us on the TV coverage? We actually got captured on camera! Only for a few seconds, but it definitely was us.'

'No, I didn't think to record it.'

'Oh, that's a shame. Well, you can look at ours some time.'

'Thank you. Kitty, I have to go now, but I'll see you on Thursday. Shall we say nine o'clock in the woods?'

After Kitty had said goodbye she sat staring thoughtfully at the phone for a moment. Then she shrugged and got up to put a load of washing into the machine.

*

Once again, the white car in the woods. Once again, Malcolm's lanky form standing by the side of it while he limbered up. What a journey we've been on since I first saw him here in January, thought Kitty.

'I'm sorry I'm a bit late,' she said. 'I normally run to here from the pub so it doesn't take very long. I tried that today but I couldn't persuade my body to do it. So I had to do a brisk walk.'

They decided to continue with a short circuit consisting of a brisk walk first, and then hopefully a bit of jogging on the way back. Malcolm said that he had tried a short run yesterday and confessed that he too couldn't manage it. 'Our bodies must be really depleted,' he said.

Kitty agreed. 'We should be gentle with ourselves while we recover. And I don't know about you, but I've been eating like a horse these last few days.'

'Mm,' said Malcolm, not agreeing or disagreeing. 'So how are you feeling now? Still disappointed?'

'Oh, not so much now. Everyone in the pub has been saying how well I did – mainly because Rob keeps on boasting about me, telling anyone who'll listen that I'm his brave girl. And I do know what I did was all wrong, of course. It was going too fast in the first half, wasn't it?'

'Common beginners' mistake, apparently. Just as well that we met the chocolate man. Or rather he met us.'

'And jelly-baby lady.' They both laughed at the memory.

'We can laugh now', said Malcolm, 'but I was really worried about you. It was so dramatic the way you just lost it.'

'It was scary, wasn't it. I couldn't think straight. And, Malcolm, I can't thank you enough for getting me through and not going on without me. I don't know what I would have done if you hadn't been

150

there.'

'My dear Kitty, I would never have left you. But if I hadn't been there, you would have got through somehow. You wouldn't have given up.'

They continued on their trek through the woods. It was a mild day and Kitty peeled off her outer layer and knotted it around her waist. Her eyes opened to delicate moss covering tree trunks and buds fattening and unfurling on branches. The branches themselves made an intricate pattern against the sky. All this and I never really noticed while we were running, she thought.

'It's different,' she said. 'I *feel* different. It's the same route, the same us, yet it doesn't seem the same now. Today I'm noticing things. I'm looking around me.'

'Is that because we don't have any particular aim today? Before we were so driven, and we were concentrating on the distance we had to cover. Of course, we had all those in-depth conversations too.'

'True. Plus most of the running was in the cold of winter. It's actually Spring now,' said Kitty in some wonderment. 'Look,' she said, pointing to the ground under the trees, 'There's primroses growing over there.'

'And no mud,' added Malcolm.

They turned round and started their laboured jog back, forcing their unwilling legs to loosen up.

'It's more than all that,' said Kitty after a moment. 'More than the changing of the seasons. I feel... I don't know, a sense of anti-climax. I don't mean because I didn't do a sub-four. But the Marathon made me dig deep inside myself, and for all those weeks it was my main focus. It took over my life, really. And now it's all over, it's like there's this gap. Well, it's all over until the next one. Maybe one in the Autumn? What do you think?'

'Malcolm?'

He slowed down to halt and turned to look at her. 'Kitty,' he said. 'I want to talk to you.'

*

'Can I have my chocolate now, please Dad?'

Malcolm loaded the last of the Cash & Carry shopping into the boot of the car. 'I'm afraid Mum said not. She said you'll be having your lunch early today.' He looked at Danny as he stood by the side of the car, scuffing a stone with his shoe, and he almost wavered. But the last thing he wanted was friction with Kitty so he added, 'Sorry, pal. That's how it is.'

He pulled out of the car park and glanced at Danny's petulant face in the rear view mirror. 'You're having an early lunch because as soon as Mum's finished in the kitchen you're going with her to Tina's to play with Luke. That'll be good, won't it? I expect you'll have some cake there. And anyway, you'll be eating loads of chocolate Easter eggs on Sunday.'

Danny didn't say anything but Rob could see he had brightened at the thought of Easter eggs. 'Will Mum be back when we get home?' he said.

'I honestly don't know. She'll be back before midday though, to start work in the kitchen.' Rob frowned in irritation as he recollected their conversation. He had asked her, as casually as he could, how long she and Malcolm were going to be out. He had nursed a vague hope that he could pop in to see Celia. But she had shrugged and said they didn't have a plan, so she could be one hour, two hours, who knows. The next frustration was that Ma had taken herself out, all dressed up, so there was no-one to look after Danny anyway. So he gave it up as a bad job. At least he'd got the Cash & Carry over and done with so he could put his feet up this afternoon.

When he had driven past Malcolm and Celia's house on the way to the Cash & Carry he had seen Malcolm's car still on the drive. So he hadn't yet left to run with Kitty. In a strange way this comforted him, because he couldn't have seen Celia anyway. Now, as they were driving back an hour and a half later, he expected to see that the white BMW was gone. Which it was. But there was another vehicle parked on the drive. It was an Estate Agent's van, and a man was erecting a 'For Sale' sign in the garden.

Chapter 13

It was hard to settle to do anything. Malcolm had tidied up a few things in the garage, he had inspected the garden, and he had glanced through the newspaper. Now he ambled through the house, only half noticing the ache in his legs. Twice he had heard a car slow down and braced himself because he thought it was Celia coming back, but no. this was the first Monday morning he had been in this house and not at work, and it felt odd. In fact he wished he was at work and that this was a normal day.

When she did come back he didn't actually hear the car at all. He only realised she was home when he looked out of the living room window and saw her opening the boot to retrieve the shopping. He hurried out to help her, aware that his legs weren't responding very quickly. But she declined his help and took the two bags herself, telling him that she normally managed perfectly well on the bus.

He stood and watched while she unpacked the bags onto the kitchen counter. Milk, fresh vegetables, fruit. Some meat, which he thought was steak, in a package. Flour, eggs and a pack of ground coffee. He picked up the pack of coffee and opened the cupboard to put it away. She took it out of his hand and put it into the fridge. He asked if he should put the kettle on and she said that would be nice. He waited for the kettle to boil, listening to its crescendo, while she continued to stow the food away. He thought how efficient she was. It would have taken him twice as long.

The kettle clicked off. 'It's always you who does the shopping,' he said.

'Well, you're usually working. And I like shopping. It gives me something to do.' Her tone was brisk.

He made two coffees, instant, and put them both down on the

kitchen table. Celia folded up the plastic carrier bags and put them in a drawer. She picked her cup up to take it to the worktop, but he asked her if she would sit down with him. After a pause, she did.

'How are you feeling now?' she said, after a moment. He wondered if she really cared, or if she only said it to fill the silence.

'Fine, considering. My body is tired and I don't have a lot of energy, but that's to be expected. After all, I did run more than twenty-six miles yesterday.'

She went to get up but he put his hand onto her arm.

'What is it? I was only going to get some biscuits.'

'Leave it. We need to talk, Celia.' He felt his heart beating in sluggish thumps. It would be easy, so easy, to go and read, or to spend the day pottering about as if it were a Sunday afternoon, leaving her to do her own thing. To co-exist in the same house like they always did nowadays.

'What do you want to talk about?'

'Us.'

Immediately he saw her face close down and she withdrew from him in her usual way. That hardened his resolve. He'd rehearsed it. Of course he'd rehearsed it. The calm laying out of the reasons, the way things were between them, nothing too emotional. But when it came to it he just blurted it out.

'I can't stand it anymore. I can't live like this. I can't seem to reach you. You freeze me out, these last few weeks especially, and I don't know what to do.'

She didn't answer. She lowered her eyes to where her hands, inert and soft, rested on the table, motionless.

'Did you hear me?' He wanted to take one of the soft hands and shake it until it came to life.

'Yes, I heard you,' she said, still not looking at him.

'I want to talk to you. *Really* talk to you. To find out why, why you're pushing me away all the time. Because Celia, if you continue to be like this...' He paused, not wanting, at the last, to say the words. After a deep breath he added, 'If we can't get our marriage back on track, then it's going to be best if we part.'

She got up quietly and went to the kitchen window, standing with

154

her back to him. He too looked out of the window. There were two sparrows playing in the bird bath, splashing and shaking their feathers in mad pleasure. Then something spooked them and they flew off. If he had to leave and live in some miserable flat, he wouldn't see birds visit his garden. But there wasn't much more that he would miss.

She turned to him. 'Why do you *think* I'm like this?' Her voice was low, but the suppressed anger was unmistakeable. 'It's all very well for you, you go to work, you have your running, you have your garden. What do I do all day?'

His anger met hers. 'Well, what did you do before we moved here? Surely you have... I don't know, your embroidery, your cooking. Those sorts of things. And you talked about joining the Women's Institute, but you never did.'

'You have no idea, do you? You have no idea just how utterly *bored* I am. Every day I hate getting up. I've been so bored that I even...' she broke off in mid-sentence and turned away. He saw that her was shoulders were trembling.

'Even what?'

She shook her head. 'It doesn't matter.'

When she didn't add more, he said, 'In the evenings, we could have done things together. But you never want to nowadays. Everything I tried to do, every conversation I tried to start, you threw it back in my face. I can't do any more Celia. It isn't my fault if you're bored.' He knew that he was being provocative, but at least he had got a reaction from her. Anything was better than her coldness.

'I wish we'd never moved here,' she said.

'You're the one who wanted to. You wanted a fresh start, you said. A fresh start after...' he took a deep breath. 'After David died.' He saw her flinch at the thing they never mentioned any more. He carried on. 'You thought you'd leave all the pain and sadness behind. Except it doesn't work that way, does it?'

'Stop it,' she wailed, putting her hands over her ears. 'You know I can't bear to talk about him. And now Adela's going away too. There's nothing left.'

'Adela will be back,' he said more gently, seeing how distressed she was. He stood helplessly by while she cried, willing himself to keep his arms dangling by his sides. But eventually he held her and rocked her until she quietened. He gazed bleakly over her shoulder at the pristine worktops and the carefully arranged crockery on the dresser in their tasteful and elegant house. A picture of the cramped untidiness of his brother's house slid unexpectedly into his mind.

'We don't have to stay, you know,' he said.

'What?' She disentangled herself from him and wiped her eyes with her fingers.

'We could sell up and go back, back where we belong. We could get a little two-bedroomed place.' He gestured around him. 'We don't need all this.' It was totally unpremeditated, out of God knows where. But as he said it, he knew the utter truth of it.

They gazed at each other, both wide-eyed at the enormity of the idea. Then Celia's face crumpled again. 'But you said you wanted to leave me.'

'I don't *want* to leave you. But I can't stand our life as it is.'

She swallowed. 'But what about your job? You couldn't just leave.'

He considered only for a split second. 'Oh yes, I could. I've never enjoyed it.' Suddenly he knew for certain that this was what he was going to do.

'But what would you do instead?'

Malcolm shrugged. 'At this moment, I honestly don't know. Something completely different. Perhaps I could set up my own gardening company. Look at my brother. He's never been a work slave, and they always manage and have a happy life. And a lot of fun, it seems.'

'And I could get a job,' she said. 'With a much smaller house we could manage.'

'We could. And a job would do you good.'

They continued to look at each other, mirroring backwards and forwards the dawning hope. Malcolm felt dizzy, lightheaded.

'Do you really mean it? Do you mean we could actually go back? Go home?' Her voice was full of yearning and Malcolm thought with compunction that he had not allowed himself to investigate the depth of her unhappiness.

'Yes. Yes I do mean it. We don't belong here.' He shook his head in wonderment. Another thing I hadn't let myself realise, he thought. I'd just doggedly kept going, day by day.

'So let's talk about it more tomorrow,' she said.

'No.' He was firm. 'We need to get the ball rolling today. Straightaway. Let's phone the estate agent and get this house valued.'

When she hesitated he said, 'If we wait, we'll think of all sort of reasons not to do it.'

He put his arms around her again, tentatively at first until she yielded to him.

She said 'I'm glad you don't want to leave me.'

He breathed in the scent of her hair, reacquainting himself with it. 'That was never what I wanted. I wanted my old Celia back. But there's one more thing.'

'What?'

'I would like you to get some proper help in dealing with your grief about David.'

Immediately she stiffened in his arms 'No! No, I can't.'

He held onto her while she tried to pull away. 'Yes,' he said, gently. 'You need to talk to someone.'

He felt her shake her head. 'It's too hard.'

'I know it's hard. But nothing will come right until you face this. I'll help and support you, but you have to do it yourself.'

Eventually, after he had soothed and coaxed her, she softened and agreed that she would get some professional help.

He saw that outside the birds had come again to the birdbath.

*

Kitty watched the steam rise from her plastic mug of coffee until it disappeared on the car windscreen, mingled with the steam from Malcolm's cup. He did always make the flask of coffee nice and hot.

'So you'll be moving away?' she said, her eyes still following the coffee vapour trail. 'How soon?'

'As soon as possible, really,' said Malcolm. 'This weekend we're going to go and look at houses. The Estate Agent was able to come last Monday afternoon, soon after we phoned up. They recommended that we put the house on the market straightaway, because the Easter weekend is a prime time for house hunting, apparently. So she got all the photographs taken on Tuesday, and the For Sale sign is going up today, probably as we speak. Then, once the ball gets rolling house-wise I'll give my notice in at work. We're being realistic about the asking price for the house, so hopefully it won't take too long.'

'Wow,' was all Kitty could think of to say.

'I know. I can hardly believe it myself. I went from thinking that my marriage was on the rocks to deciding to up sticks and move house, plus leave my job, all in the space of half an hour. It's totally out of character for me. I usually take ages to mull over things before I make a decision. But this…' He shook his head. 'Quite frankly, it's exhilarating.'

'Yes. I can tell you're excited.' And she could. It was written all over him, in his understated, typical Malcolm way.

'And Kitty, the best thing is that Celia has come back to me. It's still tentative at the moment, but it feels right. It's going to work out. I've even got her to talk about David a bit, and I know how hard that was for her. I remember how much you helped me to talk about him and what a release it was for me. I shall always be grateful for that.'

'I didn't do anything, really.'

'You listened.'

She buried her head in her cup while she tried to get her feelings in line. She'd had it all planned out, the two of them training together again through the summer, working towards another marathon.

'Of course, the other thing I'm grateful for is that you guided me through the marathon training.'

She managed to look at him and smile. 'Well, you guided me through the actual Marathon – dragged me more like - so we're quits there.' He smiled in response, and she realised that he looked ten years younger today. 'I'm pleased for you. I really am. But I am going to miss you.'

'And I you. You've been a true friend and I've valued every minute we've spent together. We should have recorded all the conversations we had during our long training runs.'

'But you're not leaving just yet, are you?' she said. 'We can still run together over the next few weeks, can't we?'

Malcolm hesitated. 'I think I won't, if you don't mind. You see, it

158

seems important now to spend time with Celia.'

Kitty looked out of the window to hide her sharp disappointment. Oh well, she thought. If things are going to change, I might as well get used to it now. She glanced idly at her watch. 'Oh no,' she gasped. 'I've done it again.'

'What? What time is it?'

'It's five to twelve. I didn't realise it was so late. Do you think you could give me a lift back to the pub? I'm supposed to be in the kitchen from twelve.' She hastily gathered up the flask and cups and buckled up her seat belt.

As they approached the turn to the pub she said, 'Do you remember when this happened before, weeks ago? We had lost track of time talking in the car and I was late. We pulled into the car-park and there was already a minibus there with a load of people inside. And I had to go straight behind the bar without changing or showering.' She didn't add the part about how angry Rob had been afterwards and what he had accused her of.

'Oh dear. I'm so sorry if I've made you late again. Both times it's because you've been listening to me. At least today the conversation was happier.'

For you maybe, she thought, but then chided herself for being ungenerous. 'It won't be so bad today,' she said. 'I'm in the kitchen doing the cooking, so I'll just have to do a quick change of clothes and I'm ready. And look,' she indicated the car park, 'There are no customers yet.'

She put her head round the door of the empty Lounge and called to Rob that she would only be two minutes. Upstairs as she threw on her kitchen clothes and washed her hands she wondered if Rob would be annoyed. Probably not; it was only just after twelve and it was quiet, although as she was running into the pub she had seen out of the corner of her eye a car disgorging three people. And even if Rob was grumpy about it, it wouldn't be happening again anyway. She sighed. It felt like the end of something precious. Still, she couldn't let herself dwell on it now.

'Sorry I'm a bit late,' she said as she hurried in behind the bar, tying on her apron as she went. 'Only Malcolm had some surprising news.

He and Celia are moving away. Their house is up for sale already.'

Rob had just scribbled an order for lunch down on his pad. A Babycham, a glass of white wine and a fresh pint of bitter stood on the counter in front of a middle-aged couple and a young woman. He was running the tap at the sink under the bar when he answered, so his reply was muffled. She picked up the slip of paper with the lunch order on it and headed for the kitchen. Funny, she thought, it sounded like Rob had said 'I know.' But how could he know? It was only when she was shaking frozen chips into the deep fat fryer that she worked it out.

*

'What's our Lou chattering to the landlord about, do you think?' said the woman to her husband, as she sipped her Babycham.

'I don't know. They seem to be looking and pointing at the picture on the wall. I noticed it myself when we were up at the bar. It's some woman with a medal round her neck.' He took a draught of beer and belched surreptitiously afterwards. His wife glared at him, so presumably it hadn't been surreptitious enough.

'Who is it in the picture, Lou?' said the woman when Louise came back, stuffing her purse back into her bag as she sat down.

'Hang on, let me get this receipt put away safely.' Louise tucked the small docket into the back of her diary. 'It's the landlord's wife. She ran in the London Marathon last weekend, and the picture is of her with her medal. They were on the ball to get the picture done so quickly, I must say. I like that.'

'Oh, I remember,' said the woman. 'Last time we came she was behind the bar with her legs all covered in mud and no shoes on, just socks.'

'But we did have a good meal, didn't we, Mum? You said so at the time. So did you, Dad. And anyway, I asked her about the mud, didn't I, and she said she'd been held up and arrived back late from her training, then there was that crowd of men already here waiting to be served, so she just had to get on with it.'

'It's always nice when you take us out for a meal,' said Dad. 'And this is a special treat, being in the week.'

'Are you sure it's alright for you not to be working? After all it is a Thursday,' said Mum.

'Well, I am working some of the time,' said Louise. 'Oh look, here comes our food.'

'I can't eat all these chips,' said Mum.

'Just eat as many as you feel like, Mum, and leave the rest. You wouldn't want the plate to arrive not looking full, would you?' Her eyes met those of the pink-cheeked cook, presumably hot from the kitchen, who was putting the plates down in front of them.

'I saw your picture on the wall,' Louise said to her quickly. 'Congratulations on running the London Marathon. I think that's fantastic.'

The cook thanked her and asked if they wanted any sauces.

'Last time we were here you were serving behind the bar with mud on your trousers. I must say you look a lot cleaner now,' said Mum, looking her up and down.

Louise heard Dad's sharp intake of breath. Typical Mum, she thought.

*

Rob pushed his motorbike out of the shed. He inspected the sky; there were only a few clouds. He had a dozen things he ought to be doing this afternoon ready for Good Friday tomorrow, but he needed to go out for a ride. He had to clear his head and give himself time to take it all in. The memory of the time, weeks ago now, when he called in at Celia's house to show her his motorbike invaded his head. That's when it had all started. Well, he wouldn't be going past her house today.

He was so busy manoeuvring the bike out that he didn't notice Ma coming across the yard towards him, coat on and a full shopping bag on her arm. Damn. He would have preferred not to talk to her, or anyone for that matter, right now. But it was too late now. He propped the bike on the stand and resigned himself.

'Off out for a ride are you?' she said. 'Are Kitty and Danny upstairs? I've got a new book for him from the library.'

'No, they've gone to Tina's.'

'Oh. I see. So that's why you're going out.'

'You're wrong there.'

'Gone out, has she?'

'I don't know. But anyway I'm just going out on my bike for a ride

161

on my own. I can do that, can't I?'

He felt her eyes on him and he looked away.

'What's wrong?'

'Nothing.' He knew he was going red as she scrutinised him. Why could she always do this? Here he was, a bloke in his thirties, and his mother could still make him feel as if he was as old as Danny and had just been caught stealing biscuits.

'You're up to something, I can tell. You're going to see her, aren't you?'

'No, I'm not.'

'Kitty and Danny are out of the way and you expect me to believe that?'

He knew she'd only keep on about it, like a dog with a bone, so he said, 'It's all over, if you must know.'

That stopped her in her tracks. Her eyebrows shot up. 'You finally saw sense, then and finished it? Or was it her?'

He clenched his teeth. He didn't want to be going into it all with his mother, but he knew she wouldn't stop now until she'd got it all out of him.

'They're moving away. I phoned her this morning and she told me.' He clamped his mouth shut to stop himself from adding 'so you can get off my back right now'. To his dismay he could feel himself trembling with fury. He stomped into the shed and grabbed a rag, came back and rubbed it vigorously over the metalwork on the bike while the whole miserable conversation played over again in his head. Just like that, she'd made things up with her husband and they were clearing off. No letting him down gently. No saying she'd miss him. Just a few sentences on the phone and there he was. Dismissed. Thank you for your services and goodbye. And now here was Ma, looking into his mind, seeing everything, like she always could.

For once, she didn't say anything. 'It turns out she's never been happy here and she's been hankering to get back to her old home,' he burst out. 'And so he's going to up and leave his job and take her back there. And as for muggins here...'

'Well, fancy that. That is a bit of news.'

He stood, breathing heavily, fuming under her gaze.

162

She sighed and put her shopping bag down. 'Look, lad, it was going to happen sooner or later. Her getting tired of you, that is. You were a just plaything to her – something to take her mind off things.' He winced but she didn't let up. 'Well what did you think was going to happen? It was always going to end, in the long run. Much better this way than Kitty finding out. And you don't suppose that that Celia, with all her fancy ways, would have worked like a dog alongside you the way that Kitty does, would she?'

He shuffled his feet. 'I know all that. But it was the *way* she did it, Ma. So cold, so snooty. I feel... discarded.'

'Well, that's just your male pride, isn't it?' He squirmed. Ma certainly wasn't going to pull any punches.

'Come on, let's sit down for a minute.' She sat down on the old bench that stood outside the shed and patted the seat alongside her. He sat on the edge of the seat, reluctant but obedient. 'She probably knew what she was doing, you know. Women usually do. Now that it's all lovey-dovey with her husband again, and he's going to do what she wants, she knew better than to have a long drawn out goodbye with you. Short and sharp was much better for both of you.'

Rob hung his head and didn't reply. He really didn't need his mother telling him what's what, even though part of him recognised the sense in what she said.

'Look, the sun's started to come out a bit,' she said. 'That's nice.' She settled herself back on the seat and lifted her face to the warmth. Rob groaned inwardly. All he wanted to do was get away for an hour on his motorbike. 'And anyway, I've got some big news myself. This will take your mind off things.' Her voice was as smug as her face.

He said, 'What is it?' like he was supposed to and resigned himself to hearing some local tittle-tattle.

'It's about John.'

'John? Which John?'

She tutted. 'The Major. He does have a name, you know. And, more to the point, it's about John and me.'

She was giving him a funny look, sort of expectant. He wished she'd just get on with it and tell him this news, whatever it was.

'You know how we usually sit together in the pub and talk when he comes in? Well, lately we've been seeing more of each other, going out for meals, things like that. And I've been to his house several times. Very impressive it is, I can tell you.'

Rob frowned. 'You mean… what *do* you mean?'

She rolled her eyes and sighed. 'I have to spell it out, do I? John and I are going out together. Courting, as we used to say in my day.'

'You mean you're actually… why is this the first I've heard about it?' It was outrageous. Ma couldn't go out with a man. She was…well, she was his Ma. She hadn't ever looked at anyone else since his Dad died.

She folded her hands in her lap. He could see she was enjoying every minute of this. 'This is the first you've known about it because you've been too wrapped up in yourself to notice anything else, like that I was off out more and having my hair done more often. And anyway, it's not your business. It's mine and John's.' She said it quietly, not in an uppity way, but even so, it was like a red rag to a bull.

'It certainly is my business. I care about what happens to you.' Visions of the Major turning up for Sunday lunch or trying his hand at serving behind Rob's bar popped up in his head.

'Calm down, will you. And anyway, there's more to tell you.'

He saw that her eyes were sparkling and her cheeks were flushed. It dawned on him that she did look particularly attractive today. She fixed him with her eyes and said, 'John has asked me to go and live with him and I've said yes.'

Rob slumped back against the seat, his head reeling. She wasn't joking when she said she had big news. 'You're going to move in with him – just like that? Don't you think it's a bit soon?'

'Oh, I've given it careful thought, believe me. But we get on really well, and John's a good man. We're both on our own and that doesn't seem to make sense when we could be together - one set of bills and all that. He's been rattling round in that big house ever since his wife died. We're neither of us getting any younger and I thought, why not? He'll look after me, don't you worry about that. He's a real gentleman.'

'But…' Rob floundered. He didn't know what to say, where to start. Eventually he said, 'I don't know what I'll do without you if you go. You've always been there.'

'I'm not going to be far away. John's house is only about half a mile from here. I can still see Danny and look after him sometimes. You didn't think I'd stop doing that, did you? I'd never stop seeing my boy.'

Rob sat like a rag doll. He was gobsmacked. He shook his head. 'I don't know what Kitty's going to say about this.'

Doris raised her eyebrows. 'Don't you? I do. She'll say she's glad that the old bat is going at last.'

Rob opened his mouth to protest, but then thought better of it.

'And that's another good reason for me going. It will give her, both of you in fact, more room to spread your wings without me breathing down your necks. You don't need me. You make a first-rate job of running this pub. Your Dad would be proud of you. In fact, I would say you're an even better landlord than he was.'

Rob picked his helmet up from the seat beside him and fiddled with the strap, although he couldn't really see what he was doing because his eyes were suddenly blurry. 'You've never said that before.'

'Well, I'm saying it now. And have you thought, you and Kitty and Danny can move into my cottage after I'm gone? You'll have plenty of space with the three bedrooms. Then you can rent out the flat and make some money on it.'

Rob blinked. It was all so much to take in. 'Kitty will love that. She's always saying how squashed up we are in the flat.'

'There you are, see. It's going to be good for all us.' She turned her head away from him and gazed out over the yard. For the first time in the conversation she seemed to stumble over her words. 'Kitty's a good girl,' she said at last. 'A bit headstrong, but she works hard and backs you up. She deserves this.'

They fell silent. After a while Doris said, 'You'd better be getting on with your ride or you won't have time. She stood up and ran her hand over the saddle of the bike. 'Ah, I did some miles with your Dad on this bike. I haven't been out on it for years.' Suddenly she put her hand on his arm. 'Take me out for a spin, Rob. Just down the road and back, nice and slow. Go on!'

Rob watched open-mouthed while she took the spare helmet down from its hook in the shed and wedged her head into it, new hairdo and all. She zipped her coat up to the top and pulled her gloves on.

Rob shook his head in wonderment. You had to hand it to Ma, she had guts.

'Come on then,' she said. 'What are we waiting for?'

Chapter 14

'I can't believe it's a year ago since my hen party,' said Nicola, as they pulled into the car-park.

'Almost to the day,' said Louise as she backed her car into the nearest space to the door that she could find. The spiteful wintry drizzle hit her in the face as she got out, and she shivered. At least she had glimpsed through the pub window the blaze of a log fire. She hurried round to Nicola's side of the car. 'Do you want a hand?' she said. 'It's a bit low slung. Mum and Dad are always complaining.'

'I can manage, thanks,' said Nicola as she puffed to heave her bulk out of the car. 'I'm not that helpless yet.'

The inside of *The Spinning Coins* did indeed exude warmth and cheeriness – just what you should expect from a British pub on a winter's night. Louise picked up two menus from the bar and ordered a glass of white wine and an orange juice while Nicola chose a table. The landlord, who was his usual cheery self, commented on the poor weather while he uncorked a fresh bottle of wine. Louise lowered her head and fumbled through her bag while she muttered an answer. But there was no sign of recognition on his part, and she preferred it that way. He asked if she wanted ice in the orange juice and a slice of orange. A slice of orange, indeed. They've raised their game, thought Louise. As well they might.

'It's really nice here, isn't it,' said Nicola as she took her orange juice. 'Cosy and not too posh.'

'Do you remember anything at all about when we came here for your hen night?'

'Hmm,' said Nicola. 'Not much. We had a meal here, didn't we?'

'Yes, they kept the kitchen open for us specially. And the food was particularly good. So later when this pub came up on my list, I remembered it.'

They looked at the menus. They were newly formatted on crisp, glossy card. 'Look,' said Louise, pointing to the words across the top. It gave her a thrill, every time.

'*As featured in The Good Pub Guide 1992*', read Nicola. 'It must be a great job to have, going round inspecting pubs.'

'It's rewarding when it's a pub like this, with lots of genuine atmosphere, a well-kept bar and proper home cooking.'

'I have to go to the toilet,' said Nicola suddenly. 'Yet again. This baby likes to make a pillow of my bladder.'

Louise ordered their cottage pie and fresh salmon while she was gone. As Nicola waddled back in, the landlord's wife came in to pick up their order. She and Nicola looked at each other and gave a smile of camaraderie, both pointing to each other's large bellies and then automatically putting a hand on their own. Louise couldn't properly hear the conversation, but she could imagine it – the immediate sisterhood, the membership of an elite club. For a moment she felt quite envious.

Well, well, well, she thought. That will put paid to her marathon running for a while. But she looks glowingly happy, and so does her husband. That's the other thing that makes a good pub. It's the people.

Lightning Source UK Ltd.
Milton Keynes UK
UKHW02f0006120918
328751UK00007B/264/P